Keeled Over at the Cliffside
Saltcliff Mysteries
Book 1

Nancy Stewart

Copyright © 2024 by Nancy Stewart

All rights reserved.

No part of this book may be reproduced in any form or by any electronic or mechanical means, including information storage and retrieval systems, without written permission from the author, except for the use of brief quotations in a book review.

Cover credit: Kelly Lambert Greer

Editing: Michelle Krueger

Chapter One

My blocky heels clicked in a satisfying way through the parking lot outside the squat, wide building where I worked just outside Washington DC. My service dog, Taco, trotted happily at my side, his nails clicking on the asphalt. Every day was a good day when you were a Labrador. If only life for humans was as straightforward.

"Morning, Ms. Vale." The security guard greeted me without looking up when I swiped in and proceeded through the turnstile. He needed only to see my clearance pop up on the screen in front of him to know it was me. I wondered sometimes if someone else could simply swipe my card and walk on by. They'd have to have a service dog at their side, of course.

"Morning Sam," I returned, feeling the tiniest bit nostalgic, knowing this would be the last time we'd engage in this little ritual. Not that Sam and I were friends, exactly. I didn't have many of those, so maybe the man who checked my ID each day was closer to my heart than he was for most people. But there was no point being nostalgic now. This life was coming to an end.

I made my way to my office, unlocking it with the key I'd have to surrender shortly, and sat down to pull the letter I'd composed over the weekend up on my screen to print. Taco curled up on the cushion in the corner of my office.

"Time for work, Taco," I said, echoing the words I'd said to him every day for the past four years—since he'd come to me as a newly trained allergen-sniffing service puppy. I let my eyes scan the words I'd written once more, doing my best not to feel remorse at leaving.

After all, I loved my job.

Well, love was perhaps too strong a word.

But I was very good at my job. And people depended on me. And I liked that. No one really depended on me outside of work except Taco Dog. But here, in service to the US Department of Defense, I was needed. I created highly technical reports that the decision makers at the top depended upon. I was respected. I was—

"Dolly! Dolly Madison. Glad you're here. What's up, dog?" Steve Donhower stood in my doorway, his too-square jaw frozen in that half smile he seemed unable to alter. The last little bit of his greeting was directed at Taco and followed with a nasal chortle. Then his face shifted and he fixed his beady eyes on me. "Colonel Divot is coming in at ten and I'm gonna need you to walk him through that report you showed me Friday. No one else gets it, frankly."

I didn't especially like Steve, but I struggled to maintain a placid expression. Steve pushed work off onto other people and was unqualified for his position, which was just above my own here at the contractor we both worked for. I suspected Steve had found his way to his position mostly thanks to his possession of a certain piece of anatomy I lacked. That, and because his father was a principal at the firm.

I needed to let him know I wouldn't be working here any more, that I'd had a major life shift and would be leaving town—the state, in fact—immediately. "Steve, I—"

"Hey, Dolly, you didn't happen to bring in any of those cookies today, did you?" Steve looked around my office, as if there might be a pastry case he'd missed upon first entering. I had a habit of stress-baking, so the office was usually the place I offloaded the extra treats. But in the last couple days, I'd been too stressed even to bake—something I hadn't realized was possible before I'd gotten the news that changed everything about my life.

"Sorry, no. No cookies today. And please, Steve, I've asked you several times to call me Dahlia. It's more—"

"Profesh. Gotcha, Ms. Parton." He actually made a fake gun with his hand and winked at me as he pretend-shot it at me.

"Yes. Professional." I sighed. Maybe leaving wouldn't be so bad. "Also, Steve?" I called him back as he turned from my office door. "I was just printing this up..." I reached for the letter of resignation on the printer.

"You can show me whatever that is later—"

"No, actually, I can't." The grief and stress and general anxiety were building inside me and forced my voice a bit higher than usual. High, but forceful, nonetheless.

Steve froze and his mouth actually fell open a tiny bit. Forceful was not a word people would generally use to describe me. Shy? Yes. Mousy? Unfortunately. Introverted? Yep. But today, I really needed Steve to listen to me. I didn't have much time and I felt like I was closing in on an emotional breaking point.

I picked up a pen off my desk and signed the letter with a flourish, handing it to him. "I won't be able to meet with Colonel Divot today. I'll be gone."

"You'll be... what?"

"I have to resign. Effective immediately." I had practiced this with Taco at home, finding the perfect balance of detail without divulging an unprofessional level of family information.

"But, but... why?" Steve looked more shocked and upset than I'd anticipated, his big jaw hanging open as he looked between the letter and me. "I can be more profesh, Dahlia. I can, I promise."

Steve sounded more sincere than I'd ever heard him,

and it was the first time he'd used my proper name. Those tiny improvements would have made a big difference a week ago. But now? I didn't have a choice.

I crossed my arms over my chest, hoping to contain a bit of the rush of emotion that was jolting around inside me as I tried to summon the words I'd rehearsed. "My sister," I began, and then to my horror, I felt my eyes fill with tears. I sniffed, took a deep breath and tried again. Surely I could simply decide not to cry. Couldn't I? I was strong. I could control myself. This was why I'd practiced. Crying at work would be unacceptable.

Taco rose from the corner and came to stand next to me, leaning gently against my leg. His version of a reassuring pat.

I had practiced this at home without getting horribly upset, but speaking the words to Taco's soft furry face hadn't been preparation enough for the reality of having to tell another actual person that my only sister—my twin sister—was gone.

"Your sister?" Steve took a step forward, his face softening as he realized the nature of my news.

"My twin sister died of cancer. It was very sudden. She has a... a..." Oh no, the tears again. One actually slid down my cheek and I rushed to wipe it away. I blurted the rest. "She has a daughter in California who has no one else. I have to go."

"Of course you do," Steve opened his arms as if he

believed I might step in for a hug, and I took a step back, finally finding the steel in my spine. Hugging people was not my favorite activity at the best of times. Hugging a man who routinely called me Jolly Dolly was not on my agenda today. Probably not ever.

"So you see, I am offering my resignation. My flight is at one."

"Today?" Steve looked surprised again.

"My niece needs me." It was true. My family was small. It had been me and my sister, who for a decade had made a strict habit of not speaking to one another, but she had evidently realized in death that I was her only option in terms of guardianship material.

"You're going to California to get your niece," Steve said, recovering his bravado slightly. "So you'll be back."

I shook my head. "No, Steve. I will not be back. I also inherited guardianship of my sister's inn on the coast. Until I can figure out what to do with it, and with her daughter, I'll be living there."

"But you have a security clearance," Steve said, apropos of nothing.

"Yes. I do." The emotion was beginning to recede and I felt stronger. I patted Taco's head and he grunted softly.

"But we'll have to read you out." Steve said this as if it would be a nearly impossible feat.

I nodded. I just hoped handling all the administrative

details that would allow me to depart wouldn't take too long.

Eventually, the security team had read me out of the projects for which I'd been cleared, taken my badges and keys, and my files and computer, and I'd left the office feeling oddly like I'd never worked there at all. Strangely, it wasn't an unpleasant feeling. In an odd way, I felt lighter. More free.

How strange to be untethered from the one thing I had any actual connection to. And what a sad statement on my life here. I swallowed down any remorse—you couldn't change who you were, after all—and I girded myself to get through this day.

I went home and gathered my packed bags. Taco Dog looked slightly more professional when he was wearing his "service animal" vest, which was his usual travel attire. Of course, that was only true if you disregarded the time he'd worn the vest while chasing after the tennis balls on the bottom of an elderly lady's walker... Taco didn't like to discuss that. He was a service dog. Just not the best behaved, perhaps. But he could sniff out a peanut or a pea like nobody's business, and that was all I really needed him to do. Legumes and I were not friends.

I looked wistfully around the hastily packed apartment I'd called home for the last decade. Again, that odd feeling of lightness filled me. I was almost... relieved?

I'd lived here, in this apartment, working the same job

as a technical analyst in the same office with the same people for ten years. And for most of that time, I had enjoyed it. Even if it had been a bit lonely.

I'd never been good at making friends—that was my sister's domain. And when we'd lived near one another, her friends were my friends. And she'd been my best friend. But when things... happened... she left me and took her bright, full life with her. I'd done my best to create a full life for myself, but it turned out I didn't have much of a knack for it. And for the most part, that was okay.

Sure, now and then I looked around and wondered if I might not be happier with a little more interaction. But since Taco had arrived four years ago, I'd been happily occupied and hadn't really felt alone. He was a good friend.

The flight to California was uneventful, as all the best flights are. Taco was very well behaved and only moderately drooly when one of the flight attendants gave him a treat. He didn't try to disassemble anyone's mobility assistive device this time, so that was a definite improvement over our last trip.

I had no trouble finding a ride and navigating the coastal highway to the tiny town of Saltcliff on the Sea, where my twin sister had run a quaint bed and breakfast for the last ten years of her life. An inn I'd never been invited to visit or even seen, except on the inn's site online.

Maybe it was the flowing curves of the seaside road,

maybe it was the salt air or the sunshine, but that feeling of lightness hit me again and even grew as I neared Saltcliff. By the time I led Taco and rolled my suitcase through the gate in front of the inn, I was managing my stress and uncertainty well. To most, I probably looked like I was on the edge of a breakdown, but for me, this was practically ebullient.

All those good feelings departed immediately upon meeting my niece, Diantha Vale.

Chapter Two

"Let's go in," I had just suggested to Taco, and we headed down the gravel path toward the front door of the inn, which was set back under a pale yellow stone archway. The entire structure appeared to have sprung naturally from the landscape, like a country cottage—a big one—from a fairy tale. The roofline curved and swooped, shingles curving right along with it, like something you might find in the Shire, where the hobbits lived. The building was two stories, all pale yellow stone with some darker bits, and the windows were arched and divided into charming panes, the borders painted in a pale green color.

An enormous tree leaned close to the front of the building, a gnarled and twisted limb supporting a swing that hung just next to the inn's facade.

"You must be her." There was a smallish person sitting on the swing, though I'd only just noticed her, camouflaged as she was in silence, stillness, and a getup that made me wonder if bank robbing was part of her daily routine.

I pulled myself up a bit straighter. I was a her. But was I "her"? Yet to be determined.

Taco Dog dropped his tail end and let his tongue loll out one side of his mouth as he watched the person hop off the swing and approach. He let out a gentle whine of greeting.

"And you would be...?" I lifted my sunglasses to peer down at the person, who was smaller than I'd initially thought.

"I'm Danny."

Danny. "Diantha?"

"Like I said. Danny."

Well.

My niece Diantha had a beautiful face with a pert little nose that reminded me exactly of my sister Daisy's. She also had smears of chunky eyeliner surrounding her eyes, lipstick that was nearly black, and a ring in one nostril. Her short, DIY haircut fell around her face in locks that were black tinged with both blue and green, and her short black dress might have had a first life as a flour sack—do they make those in black? From its hem descended two skinny, shredded-fishnet-clad legs. Her feet were hidden by enormous, thick-soled black shoes.

"You're staring," she said.

Taco let out a little groan, as if apologizing for me.

"Yes, sorry. I am. I apologize. I believe I'm your Aunt Dahlia."

"You don't know who you are?" Diantha asked, one side of her dark lips quirking up. "Do you know who this is?" She extended a hand, palm up and fingers curled inward, toward Taco. He leaned his nose forward, accepting her greeting.

"Yes, of course. This is Taco Dog."

"You named your dog Taco?"

"Taco Dog," I said again.

"Isn't it a little extra to name your dog 'Dog'?" Now both sides of the girl's lips tilted into a smile and both her hands planted themselves into Taco's excessively furry ruff as she dropped to her knees in front of him. Taco, the traitor, groaned in delight and nuzzled the girl's face.

I cleared my throat, uncertain what the next move should be. Sometimes I envied my dog, who suffered no such uncertainties. He leaned into my niece's arms until he finally lowered his head to the ground and flopped down onto his back, exposing his belly for her to scratch.

"Is he really a service dog?"

"He is, and you're really supposed to ask before you pet someone else's dog. You had no idea if he might be vicious."

Diantha laughed at that as Taco let out an indignant groan. He was the furthest thing from vicious there was.

But still.

None of this was going at all the way I'd imagined. In the last photo I'd seen of my niece, she wore a little pink pinafore and mary janes on her tiny feet. Of course, she'd been two in that photo. But I hadn't been prepared for this... what did they call this look? Goth? Emo? I didn't know, but it assured me that I was utterly unprepared for the task I'd taken on here.

"Well, it seems I will be your guardian now, Diantha," I tried.

The girl froze, just for a second, as if the words had hit something deep inside her she hadn't realized she'd left unprotected. But then she stood and brushed off her knees, lifting her little heart-shaped face in a defiant motion.

"Right," she said, and then she turned and headed for the front door of the inn.

"Well, okay. Come, Taco." I followed her, wishing I had a better sense for exactly what was supposed to come next in this process. There'd been no briefing or directions sent ahead. Just the lawyer's call, the address, and the suggestion to settle in at the inn before our meeting Tuesday for lunch.

I stepped through the heavy wood door into what appeared to be a living room. Since the inn had once been a home, it made sense.

A fire glowed low in a fireplace against the far wall, and the room was scattered with comfortable-looking furniture—armchairs and low tables, couches and ottomans. There were side tables with glowing lamps, and the walls were covered with volumes of books tucked into dark wooden built-in bookcases.

Diantha was nowhere to be seen.

I let out a little aggravated sigh and let go of my suitcase. "Hello?" I called. No one answered, and the picture window on the far side of the room drew my eye. Taco and I stepped closer. Outside the big window was a patio scattered with tall heating stands and tables and chairs. Beyond the patio was the sea. The Pacific Ocean, to be exact.

It hurled itself lazily against rocky cliffs on either side of a wide pale beach. People ran and walked along the sand, dogs following at their heels or chasing ahead of them. The sun glinted off the green-blue surface of the water as waves broke near shore, carrying surfers atop a few of them. Despite the beachy scene, the air outside had held a chill, and I gave an involuntary shiver, thinking of those souls out there riding waves in wetsuits. Too cold for me, certainly.

It was on the heels of this thought that a voice greeted me.

"Hello, there. You must be Dolly."

I swallowed back the automatic correction I made whenever anyone shortened my name, and turned to address a tall, thin, dark-skinned woman with the most elegant posture I'd ever seen. I immediately straightened, suddenly self-conscious in my own stance. The woman was beautiful in an understated way, and though I tried hard to decide, it was impossible to know if she was thirty or seventy years old. She had an ageless grace I knew I didn't share, and I felt suddenly self-conscious in her presence. Which, of course, made no sense at all.

"Hello. Yes, I'm Dahlia. Daisy's sister."

The woman reached out a long-fingered hand, clasping my own. "I'm so sorry for your loss. Daisy was a wonderful woman. One of my dearest friends. Very special to me." A tear gathered in the corner of one of her eyes and slid silently down her cheek, as if it didn't want to interrupt what she was saying.

"Then I am sorry for your loss," I said, feeling like an imposter for accepting condolences for a sister I barely knew.

The woman bowed her head a moment, and then lifted her dark eyes to me again with a smile. "I'm Amal. I am the manager here. Or, I was... I mean..." the smile faltered. "Depending, of course, on what you intend to do with the inn."

I retrieved my hand from Amal's, feeling awkward as usual, but rushed to reassure her. "I know next to nothing about running an inn. I believe your job is quite secure." Taco Dog nosed forward, clearly feeling left out. "This is Taco."

Amal smiled and her shoulders dropped a bit, though

she still stood at least six inches taller than my perfectly average five foot, three. She gazed at Taco and reached out a hand to let him sniff before looking back up at me.

"May I show you around?" Amal asked. "I've done my best to clear some space in your sister's rooms for you."

"Thank you."

Amal led me to a big door to one side of the central seating area. She knocked lightly on the door, and then twisted the knob, pushing the door inward. We stepped in, and more of my sister's life was revealed. We stood inside what appeared to be a house in a house.

"Your sister and Diantha live here," Amal said, catching herself. "Lived here. You'll live here, I mean." Her eyes brushed mine, looking painfully sad for a split second, and then she took a deep breath and led me farther inside.

The space was less formal than the inn's living areas, but no less cozy. Oversized chairs and a long sectional couch took one corner of the room, while three doorways stood closed just past a small dining area. A kitchen was visible beyond the dining room.

"Diantha's room," Amal gestured to the first closed door. "Bathroom," she pointed at the second and then moved over to open it. I gazed within. Not entirely modern, but certainly functional. "And your room here." Amal opened the third door and a familiar scent wafted out as I stepped closer.

I hadn't seen Daisy in years, but the air inside her room

took me back to childhood. It smelled of her somehow. Nothing I could put my finger on, but it was the essence of nostalgia moving through the space. Taco whined and I felt tears pressing in the back of my throat.

"I'll give you a few minutes to get settled and then we can tour the rest of the inn?" Amal said, seeming to know I needed a moment. "I'll go get your bag."

She disappeared, and Taco and I stood in the center of my sister's room. In the center of her life, really. I was an imposter and a misfit in every conceivable way. But somehow, I'd have to make this work. For Diantha. For Daisy, too, I guessed. For all the sisterly things she wanted that I was never able to give her.

For a moment, I stood still, some idea that Daisy was here with me taking space in my mind. But she was not, I knew that. My twin sister was gone. And I had never gotten to say so many of the things I'd wanted to say. Things I'd needed to practice, to think about far from the moment in which they were required.

Taco sat down and I stepped to the dresser, examined the items lining its top—a jewelry box, a small wooden elephant, a glass bottle holding an amber liquid. I looked up into the mirror that hung over the dresser, seeing myself but also seeing my sister. We'd never been identical—not in our genes or in our ways of being in the world. Daisy was beautiful—wide-eyed, blond, and tan-skinned. She got along easily with other people and always seemed to know what to say. My own brown hair did little to set off the sallow tone of my skin or my light brown eyes. And when it came to people? Well, books were always much easier for me to understand. I'd always thought maybe Daisy's life was easier. Although for many years, she used her innate understanding of the world—of people—to make my life easier too. As I stared at my reflection, I could almost see her there at my side, and my heart twisted inside my chest.

Being in her room, in her life, made it all real in some ways. Surrounded by her things, I felt closer to my sister than I had in many years. I was about to leave the room and its dusty yellow walls when a photograph hung next to the door caught my attention. It was us—my sister and I. Moving closer, I recognized the shot. It had been taken at Grandmother's farm, the two of us sitting on the steps of the broad porch. Daisy and I wore sundresses, our knobby ten-year-old knees pushing from the hems as we sat side by side. My gaze was fixed on the camera, solemn and serious, but Daisy's eyes were on me, her mouth open in a laugh and her arm flung around my shoulders. My sister had been my very best friend for so long... the photo created a heavy feeling inside me, as if I'd been holding a rock within that I'd only just noticed.

"Oh Daisy," I whispered, tracing one finger down her cheek. Taco let out a little whine behind me, and I turned to him. "Let's look around."

I wandered the rooms, avoiding Diantha's, since the

heavy beat of music suggested she was inside, though I couldn't imagine what pre-teens with dark eyeliner did alone in their rooms these days. I doubted she was talking on the phone endlessly as Daisy had done, nor working on a scale reproduction of the Titanic as I'd spent several years doing in my free time before graduating high school.

As I stepped back into the living room, Amal reappeared, pulling my suitcase behind her.

"I'll just put this in your room." She did as promised, and then nodded toward the door that led back into the lobby of the inn.

I followed as she led, and pulled the door shut behind me, gazing around the empty lobby as a shiver passed through me.

"Amal?"

She turned, her eyes friendly.

"Are there no guests?"

"Ah, not now, no. We cleared the books for a few weeks as Daisy..." Amal's eyes flooded with tears and then she blinked purposefully. "We thought it would be best. But guests will begin checking in again this weekend."

"I see," I said, and nodded to indicate that we could proceed with the tour.

Amal took me through two guest rooms on the main level and four more upstairs, each of which had its own bathroom and cozy furnishings. "Each room is named for a character of one of Daisy's favorite books," Amal explained, pointing to the nameplate on the door of an upstairs room as we pulled it shut. So far, I'd noticed Alice, Holden, and Gandalf. I'd had no idea Daisy cared for fiction. Interesting.

Eventually, we found ourselves back in the kitchen of the little house where I'd live with Diantha. Amal explained that guests were given extensive breakfast offerings each morning, usually laid out in a buffet style in the dining room that lay just off the main lobby.

"I see," I said, glancing longingly at the double ovens and sprawling center island, which was topped with a gorgeous butcher block that was clearly not just for show. My brain was spinning. I was tense and nearing overwhelm with so much new and unfamiliar in such a short period of time. When I was overwhelmed at home, I baked. Often in very large quantities.

"Who prepares the breakfast?" I asked.

"Daisy did for a while," Amal said. "But when she got sick, Danny and I helped."

"You manage quite a lot here, I guess."

Her eyes dropped mine, and she put an elegant hand flat on the countertop as if to brace herself. She nodded. "Daisy was... she was special to me. I would have done... I mean, I was happy to help."

"Danny cooks, then? Does she receive compensation for her work here?"

Amal looked up and her eyes narrowed slightly, and

then she said, "No, Daisy believed it was important to pitch in where you were needed, and I guess Danny realized she was needed in here."

"I will do the baking," I said, realizing it had been more of an announcement only when Amal's eyebrows rose swiftly.

"Oh, no, you don't need to—"

"I would very much like to do the baking," I tried again. I knew I'd need something to steady me through this transition, and this kitchen was calling to me already.

"Oh, okay, well..."

"I'm an excellent baker."

"I have no doubt, it's only—"

"Daisy told you about the coffee cake?" There had been an early baking incident when we were very young. I'd been a bit too literal as I improvised a recipe once when we were five or so. But after that my baking had been faultless. Mostly.

"No," Amal said slowly. "Just... are you sure you don't need me?"

"You have enough to do, I'm guessing, since I haven't the first idea how to manage guests and payments and whatever else we do here."

She nodded slowly, her thin lips pulling into a smile. "All right, then."

"I'll practice over the next few days if you'll help me

understand what the requirements will be for quantities and variables."

"Ah, sure," Amal said.

"And if Diantha can continue to help, that would be ideal."

"She is a little bit..."

I cocked my head, waiting. What was my niece, exactly?

"Well, she's sad, as you can imagine. We might want to give her a bit of space for a while."

I nodded. I would do some research. I wasn't sure if space was the best idea, or if a more hands-on approach to guardianship would be better. "All right."

"Well," Amal said. "There is plenty of food in the refrigerator. People have been dropping off casseroles for days. If it's all right with you, I'll just head home and return tomorrow to begin showing you the ropes a bit."

I nodded. "That's fine. Diantha and I have lunch tomorrow with the attorney, also."

Amal smiled and excused herself, and I rolled up my sleeves after settling Taco in a corner. I needed to bake.

Chapter Three

"Diantha, are you ready?" I stood at the door to the apartment calling back to the closed door of Diantha's bedroom where the music coming from the crack beneath the door was now some kind of caterwauling female voice. I preferred the throbbing bass of the previous evening, but I also believed strongly in silence.

Taco whined, and looked up at me. "You try," I told him.

Taco trotted to Diantha's door and sat, lifting a paw and scraping it repeatedly down the bottom pane of the wooden door. After a moment, the music stopped and the door opened.

"Oh hello there," Diantha said, reaching to pet Taco.

"Diantha, we need to meet the lawyer now."

She glanced past Taco to me and rolled her eyes. "I don't want to go listen to him drone on about irrelevant details in that pretentious new restaurant. Why couldn't he just come here?"

I didn't know the answer, so I simply waited.

"Fine." She straightened and stomped toward me, Taco following her. "Is Taco coming?"

"Of course. He goes where I go. Especially to places where I might be inadvertently poisoned."

"This place is the fanciest spot in town. No one would ever be poisoned there—it would ruin their chances of getting a Central Coast Star."

"What is that?" We headed out the back door of our apartment and made our way to the sidewalk that led up Nutmeg, the main street through the center of Saltcliff.

"I don't know," Diantha moaned, taking Taco's leash from my hand. "Some big deal award for food or whatever that Chef Tippen is super mad about."

"Who is Chef Tippen?"

"He's the chef at the other super duper fancy place in town, the one that's been everyone's favorite forever. He's always gotten the Star, and now this new place is going to take it away from him, I guess."

"Well, the food must be quite good at the Cliffside. It was the place Mr. Franklin suggested first."

Diantha was silent a moment and then, in a voice quite different from the defiant and assertive one she generally used, said, "Mom really wanted to eat there. We never got the chance."

Oh.

Daisy.

I'd spent the previous night finding myself inordinately sad about Daisy. But I had to dig deep to understand the special brand of grief I felt because it wasn't entirely rational to grieve for someone I hadn't spoken to in a decade. Was it? Instead, I allowed myself to be sad for the sister I'd once known—the twin who was the brighter half of me. When we were small, Daisy was the one who intuitively understood how the world operated in a way I just couldn't fathom. She'd been my guide. And then she'd abandoned me.

I was sad too. And I understood—abstractly, at least—how Diantha might be feeling.

"Maybe we could consider this lunch a kind of tribute to your mother?"

The girl looked up at me, dark-smudged eyes narrowed a bit. "What do you mean?"

"Well, maybe we can work to remember her actively while we are there. Eat things she might like, try to honor her memory in our experience?" Oh, that sounded good. I was proud of those words—a rare occurrence for me when it came to empathy, etcetera.

"Okay," Diantha said, her voice soft again. "She would like that. She liked seafood a lot."

We walked in silence down the wide sidewalk on one side of Nutmeg. We passed a number of similarly styled shops and eateries, all beckoning us inside with crafty window displays highlighting sweet treats or new book releases or skeins of soft-looking yarn. I noted Saltcliff Chocolates and Seabreeze Sweets, both piping the scents of chocolate and taffy from their storefronts in a way that made my stomach growl. Tidal Beans Coffee and Tidepool Books both seemed like good places to spend a quiet afternoon, and Lighthouse Apothecary across the street was also interesting. I'd need to come back to do some exploring. But for now, we'd arrived at the Cliffside.

The restaurant had a large plate glass window facing the sidewalk, through which I could see several tables of diners. They sat at tables with white cloths, glittering glassware, and more forks than seemed necessary for a lunchtime meal. We stepped inside to the strains of light classical music and the tinkling of cutlery against plates.

"Hello there. Reservation? Oh..." The host's face dropped its solicitous smile as he spied Taco. "I'm afraid we don't allow animals inside. You might try the Barkcliff Diner over on Ginger."

"Taco is a service dog," I explained. "He is sensitive to any allergens that might cause a reaction."

His face remained blank.

"So I don't die while I eat here."

A dark eyebrow went up as the man gazed down at Taco, who was sniffing at the host's podium enthusiastically. "I see."

"We are meeting Mr. Franklin for lunch," I said, assuming the topic of my dog had been closed.

"Err. Well..." the host was still frowning at my service dog when a tall, thin man in an overly large suit rose from a table in the center of the restaurant. "Dahlia? Diantha. Over here." He smiled widely at us.

"I expect that's Mr. Franklin," I said, and gestured for Diantha to precede me to the table. Most of the other diners watched as Taco escorted us to our table, and pretended not to watch as I moved one chair back so that he could sit next to me. The host scurried over to remove the chair.

"Hello," I said, addressing the man in the ill-fitting suit. "Mr. Franklin? I am Dahlia Vale. This is my niece Diantha, and my service dog Taco."

"Pleasure," Mr. Franklin said, smiling widely and showing off slightly brown teeth as he waved us into our seats.

Diantha sat, gazing around at the people who were slowly returning their interest to their own plates, and we each plucked our napkins off our settings and dropped them into our laps. Before I could utter another word, a woman appeared with a pair of tongs and a platter of steaming cloths. She held one out to me with the tongs.

"Er, okay." I took it, wiping my hands with the warm cloth. Diantha glanced at me with a confused look as she accepted her own cloth and then mimicked my actions with a wrinkled nose.

"I washed my hands at home," she whispered, leaning over to me.

I nodded and was about to speak to Mr. Franklin when a long menu was dropped in front of my face by the waiter.

"Specials!" he shrilled loudly, making it clear that until the business of restauranting was done, no one else would speak.

The list was long and seafood-heavy, which was fine with me, but Diantha did not appear to be a wholly fish-friendly diner, based on her continued look of disgust.

"Thank you," Mr. Franklin told the waiter as he finished up. We ordered our drinks, and finally, were left to say hello.

"I offer you my sincere condolences first of all," Mr. Franklin said, looking at both of us. "Daisy was a wonderful woman and a great loss for the town of Saltcliff. She will be missed."

I nodded my acceptance and felt a strange little twinge in my chest as a tear slipped down my niece's cheek, which she wiped away furiously with her palm. Taco got up and moved closer to her chair, leaning into her side.

The waiter came back to inquire about our choices before anyone else managed a word.

"The swordfish special?" he asked hopefully, looking between us. There did seem to be many diners enjoying the swordfish, but the way he was pressing it made me want to go a different way. I ordered the salmon salad, and Diantha was subdued with a fried cod sandwich that came with french fries.

"Mom loved French fries," she whispered. I smiled back at her.

Our lawyer, Mr. Franklin, did opt for the swordfish, which seemed to please the waiter.

"I am allergic to legumes," I told the man before he could depart.

"Of course, madame." He turned and scurried away.

"I hope your first night at the inn was all right," Mr. Franklin said, looking at me again.

"It was fine."

"And do you have thoughts about what you plan to do with the inn in the future?"

"Does that impact our conversation today?" I asked.

"Not necessarily. The will is straightforward, and the inn is in a trust for Diantha, which she will take over when she is twenty-two. Until then, you are the guardian of both your niece and the property. But there are certainly ways you might opt to, ah, cash out, as it were."

As it were? "As it were what?"

"It's a saying. I just mean, should you want to."

"My sister wanted her daughter to have the inn, correct?"

"Yes."

I turned to Diantha. "You would like to inherit the inn?"

"I mean... yeah, I guess. I'm twelve. Who knows what I'll want when I'm twenty-two?"

"Then until she is twenty-two, I'm an innkeeper," I told them. A strange kind of lightness filled me at the statement.

Diantha was watching me with an expression I hadn't seen on her before, something between impressed and bewildered.

We hadn't been there long, but I did my best to drink a full thirty-two ounces of water each morning before lunchtime, and I'd drained my glass at the table too. I rose, causing Mr. Franklin to awkwardly push back from his chair, which made Diantha look nervously between us. "What?" she asked.

"I was just going to use the restroom before the food comes," I said, pushing my chair back in and pointing to a little hallway off the main dining room. "Will you watch Taco?"

My niece smiled at this and I headed to the back.

As I was finishing up in the bathroom, a voice came through the wall between the bathroom I was in and the one next door.

"We met yesterday morning at his place," the deep male voice said. "He doesn't have a choice. I own the majority share, and I'm buying him out. It's my restaurant either way. That frog just cooks here."

Well.

I did not think frogs were generally capable chefs, and could only assume that whoever it was must have been talking about the French chef of the restaurant we were currently in. But I wasn't sure what to make of the rest of it. I pushed the thought aside as I pulled the door open, and nearly collided with a ruddy-cheeked, sleek-suited man in the hallway.

"My bad," he said, waving a hand in front of him to indicate I should precede him back to the dining room.

"Thank you," I said, feeling an unwanted blush heat my cheeks.

I took my seat again and watched as the man sat down at the table next to ours.

Our food was delivered at the same time meals were being brought to the table next to us, where the bathroom talker sat with a few other men.

I lowered my plate to Taco's nose, and he sniffed at the same time the host did from his location just a few feet away.

Taco did his job thoroughly—and the saliva beginning to drip from his jowls was a testament to his dedication. Most labs would have happily devoured my lunch instead of checking it for me without even touching the plate.

The drool was the reason Taco wore a bib with his

service vest. I put the plate back in front of me and used Taco's bib to wipe his mouth, settling him again at my side.

"That's quite a dog," the boisterous man at the table next to ours laughed, holding up a martini in a toast. "He enjoys fine dining?"

"He's not here to eat," Diantha said, speaking before I had a chance. "He sniffs out allergens that might hurt her. He's a service dog. A really super smart one."

"How 'bout that?" the man said, returning to his own conversation.

"Good boy, Taco," Diantha said, and an odd warmth washed through me as Taco smiled up at her, a thin line of drool dripping from one side of his jowls. Since Taco was asked to sniff out allergens but rarely allowed to sample, I cut a small piece of salmon from the edge of my plate with an extra fork and slipped it to him.

I was about to ask another question of my lawyer, hoping Mr. Franklin might simply get the business matters handled so we could move on, when the man behind us spoke again, loudly enough to draw the attention of most of the other diners.

"This fish is absolutely delicious," he declared. He looked around as if his intent was, indeed, to draw the entire restaurant's eyes to his table. "Incredible. Perfect. My compliments to the chef," he added, nodding to the waiter who'd approached.

"What a turd," Diantha muttered, only loudly enough for Taco and I to hear.

I suppressed a mild chuckle. The man did seem rather full of himself.

"Who is that?" I asked Mr. Franklin.

"He's a real estate developer who lives in town," Mr. Franklin said. "John Baldwicki. He's recently announced the sale of a tract of land to a hotel conglomerate to build a resort property just south of Saltcliff. Half the town is ecstatic, the other half hates him for it."

"Why?" Diantha asked.

"It's one of those big properties with restaurants and pools, arcades and shows—it'll draw a lot of tourists."

"Isn't this essentially a tourist town already?" I asked.

"A sleepy seaside tourist town," Mr. Franklin said, holding up one finger with a smile. "I guess there's a distinct difference."

I understood the resistance, I supposed. Saltcliff did have a kind of quiet charm that might be lost if hordes of tourists crowded the sidewalks at all times.

We ate our meals in relative peace, Diantha managing to suck down at least three sodas as I ate my salad. I wondered if Daisy had restricted Diantha's soda intake. That was a thing parents did, right? I made a mental note to read a book about parenting tween girls.

As our plates were cleared, Mr. Franklin extracted a folder from his briefcase. "I'm so glad we had this opportunity to meet, Ms. Vale. I just have a few things for you to sign to finalize everything."

"Shouldn't we be doing this in your office?" I asked him. Why on earth was he handing me legal documents over the salt and pepper shakers?

"Ah, well," he smiled. "I've really wanted to try this place, and I figured it would be a fun way to introduce you to the town and get a chance to see what everyone's been so excited about. Killing two birds, as it were."

As it were again.

I read the papers he handed across, no small feat considering the number of pages. His recurrent sighing told me he had most likely expected that I would simply sign the documents, but that was certainly not my style. And a bad idea in general where legalities were concerned.

Most of the lunch crowd had cleared by the time I had finished reading. Mr. Franklin had consumed four espressos, and I'd excused my niece and Taco to walk back to the inn without me. There had been plenty of huffing and puffing from the waiter as well, who clearly would have preferred that we'd met in Mr. Franklin's office, but none of it bothered me. I would read, I would sign, and I would take on my new responsibilities carefully.

After all, I was beginning a whole new life, and now that I'd had a good night's sleep, I was feeling more settled about it.

As I handed back the last of the papers, I heard the

host gasp with what sounded like horror. I turned, curious what had flapped such a seemingly unflappable man. He held a phone to his ear.

"Sick? No. I assure you sir, it was not the food."

A pause.

"No. Not possible."

Another pause.

"Three people, you say? No."

Mr. Franklin and I exchanged a worried glance.

"Excuse me," Mr. Franklin called across the now-empty restaurant to the host, who'd stuffed his phone back into his pocket and wore a worried expression. He hurried over, looking distractedly toward the kitchen. "I couldn't help but overhear. Was someone food poisoned?"

"Of course not. They were probably sick before."

"Might I ask what they ate?"

"They say it was the swordfish, but that is utterly ridiculous. Chef Teratine is a professional. Highly regarded. Well credentialed. A Beard nominee." The host sniffed and walked away as Mr. Franklin made a worried noise.

We stood and made our way outside, where the lawyer shook my hand but stepped back abruptly. "Oh dear." His hand dropped to his stomach, and he turned rather green. "I'm afraid I'm not feeling well now."

"Probably just the power of suggestion. You'll be fine."

"I do hope so. Good day." With that, Mr. Franklin turned and all but ran to a dark sedan parked at the curb.

I walked back to the inn at a leisurely pace, contemplating the new life I was about to begin. I was able to categorize elements of the past two days and make a list of sorts in my head. I was pleased and comforted to see the line of positives growing longer. As the warm sun danced over the draping branches of pine and eucalyptus hanging from the heavily treed median in the center of Nutmeg, I decided it might have been a good thing coming here. Maybe I'd needed a new start.

Chapter Four

That night, Diantha did not disappear back into her room immediately after dinner. Instead, she joined me in the little den and flopped onto the couch. Taco followed her, settling in beside her. I almost reprimanded him—he'd never been allowed on furniture back in Virginia—but he dropped his head on Diantha's hip and she stroked his ear. They both looked so happy.

A local news program was on, and I was half-watching it as I worked on my latest project, my fingers moving almost automatically around the crochet hook and yarn.

"What are you making?" Diantha asked, peering at me. Her makeup was gone, and it was almost startling to see her this way—she was so young, I realized. Poor Daisy. Her daughter was just a kid and she'd had to go so early in her life. I felt a stirring inside me to finish what my twin had started. To do a good job.

"It's a sweater for Taco."

Diantha glanced at Taco, who looked back at her, his doggy eyebrows drawing together.

"He's awfully furry already. Does he really need a sweater?"

"It got cold where we used to live."

"It doesn't really get that cold here," Diantha said. "But Mrs. Damlin down the street has a greyhound that's really old and almost hairless now. He's the same size as Taco, and I bet he gets cold."

"I don't know Mrs. Damlin. Wouldn't it be strange to crochet a sweater for her dog?"

"You could meet her that way," Diantha suggested. "You're going to need some friends here."

Was I? I honestly hadn't had many friends in Virginia. "I'm not especially good at making friends, I'm afraid." Why not be honest with my niece? "Socialization is not my strong suit."

Diantha blew out a raspberry, making a sound that caused Taco to startle and glance up at her curiously. "I'll help. She'll love you."

I shrugged, mentally shifting the purpose of my work to Mrs. Damlin's greyhound instead of my own dog.

Just then, the news anchor spoke, drawing my attention as a picture of the Cliffside Restaurant filled the screen.

"Twelve diners were sickened today eating a meal at

the acclaimed Cliffside Restaurant in Saltcliff. While most of the diners recovered within hours, one found himself in the hospital as a result of his meal, and does not appear poised to recover soon. Medical staff have offered no further comment on the status of the man— prominent Saltcliff real estate developer John Baldwicki."

Diantha and I exchanged a worried glance. "I feel fine," she said.

"Me too," I assured her, but I thought worriedly about Mr. Franklin and his too-green expression as he left me after I'd signed the contracts.

The next morning, Amal arrived with news just after Diantha headed off to school.

"Your lunch yesterday," she said breathlessly as she flew through the front door, dropping her bag behind the check-in desk. "You were at the Cliffside, right?"

"Yes," I answered. "Is everything all right?"

She lifted a hand to her short dark hair, as if realizing she'd been running. "Well, no. You heard about the food poisoning? It was on the news last night."

I nodded.

"Well, one of the diners is dead. The only one who didn't recover from the food poisoning."

That got my attention. I stared at Amal. "Mr. Baldwicki."

"Right. John Baldwicki. A real estate tycoon."

"Oh, yes. We saw him there, actually. He was fairly..." I paused, not wanting to speak ill of the dead. "He was somewhat..." I recalled his exuberant exclamations over his food and the arrogant tone he'd used in his bathroom phone conversation.

"You mean obnoxious, probably, and you're definitely not the only one who felt that way. He wasn't a popular man around Saltcliff. Did you hear about the land development project he was trying to push through?"

"Mr. Franklin told me about it, yes."

Amal nodded, as if everything was now clear. "There are some who will say he got what he deserved."

That got my attention. I frowned at her. "But you don't think it was intentional, do you? Several people were poisoned."

She sighed. "No, I'm sure it wasn't. After all, plenty of people got sick. Maybe it was karma or something that he just got a worse case."

Amal went about her business, looking over something on the monitor attached to the registration desk, but the conversation felt unfinished somehow, and I stood still for a moment working to make my brain focus on what was bothering me.

"Dahlia?" she asked, gazing across the room at me with a concerned look on her face. "Are you all right? You're not sick too, are you?"

I shook my head, breaking the dazed state I'd fallen into as I thought. "No, sorry. Just trying to think this through."

"What?"

"Why would one diner react differently?"

"Compromised immune system?"

"Did Mr. Baldwicki have a compromised immune system?" I asked her.

Amal rolled her eyes at the ceiling and lifted a hand. "I have no idea. Does it really matter?"

It didn't. I knew it didn't... only, a man was dead. So maybe it did.

Taco, who had been lying on his side near the door to the apartment rolled up onto his stomach and groaned, giving me a stern look.

"No," I agreed. "Maybe it doesn't."

Still my brain thirsted for more information, needing on some cellular level for things to make sense, to lie flat. I unrolled the morning paper—a local edition that covered Saltcliff news on the front page. The restaurant poisoning incident was front and center, with a second article below it about John Baldwicki.

"It's in the paper," I said. "Both the poisoning and Baldwicki's death. And there's a re-run of a food critic's review."

"Was it good?" Amal asked, glancing my way.

"Actually no," I said, reading it. It had been first published when the Cliffside was originally opened. It wasn't especially glowing, but I didn't think a bad review equated to poisonous food in general.

Taco had moved to sit by the front door, a clear sign he needed to go out, so I pulled on my hat and sunglasses, and gathered his leash, turning to Amal. "I'm going to take Taco for a walk, okay?"

"Sure," Amal said, appearing relieved that we were finished discussing Mr. Baldwicki's unfortunate demise.

Only, I wasn't sure we were. My brain didn't seem ready to let the topic go, but some fresh salt air might clear my mind.

Taco and I stepped outside, heading to the front of the inn's property through the dramatic garden my sister had planted and tended. Diantha had told me that the garden had been Daisy's real love. That had been true when we were kids, too. She'd gotten her fascination with flowers from our mother, who'd taken her own obsession so far as to name her daughters for flowers. I guess that explained Diantha's rather unusual name.

I looked back through the garden gate at the riot of

color within and felt my heart tug. "Oh, Daisy," I whispered. Taco nudged my leg and then stepped ahead, encouraging me to remember that we were supposed to be walking, not mourning estranged twin sisters.

"Let's go, boy." I let Taco take the lead, and after strolling the long cliffside road facing the water and taking in the charm and beauty of the seaside cottages and mansions along the path, we wound down along an open area. It was filled with tall grass, and there was an inlet through the center of it. We walked off the edge of the paved trail, following a well-trodden dirt path through the marsh, and eventually came out on the other side, where pavement met us once again.

For a moment I stopped to admire the view—the open area framed the bay perfectly, and there were sea birds swooping and calling overhead, making me feel momentarily as if I was alone in this pristine environment.

"It's a shame, isn't it?" A raspy voice came from my side, and I jumped, having failed to notice another person nearby.

"I'm sorry?" Taco dropped to his haunches, which usually meant the person we'd encountered wasn't a threat. He sometimes growled or whined if he wasn't sure.

"The land. The resort? Surely you've heard."

"Sorry, we're new in town." I smiled at the squat little woman who wore what appeared to be a muu muu and a slouchy hat, and who had a greyhound on a leash at her side that was eyeing Taco with suspicion. "Are you by any chance Mrs. Damlin? I think we might be neighbors."

The woman took off her sunglasses and squinted up at me. "Well, I'll be. Different hair, stodgier clothes. But you and Daisy could be sisters."

"We are sisters. Uh. Were."

"I mean you could be twins!"

"We are twins. Fraternal, though."

"I'll be." Another phrase I'd never really understood.

"Yes." What else did one say to this? I shifted my weight and glanced around. "I'm Dahlia Vale. I'll be taking over the inn."

The woman nodded. "Tessa Damlin. Happy to meet you. So sorry about your sister."

"Yes. I am too."

"Well, we'll see you back in the neighborhood, I suppose!" Tessa made to leave, pulling her dog along with her, but I stopped her.

"Sorry, what is your dog's name?"

"This is Albert."

"It's very nice to meet you both," I told her. "Would Albert like a sweater?"

Ms. Damlin gave me an odd look, tilting her head to one side. "A sweater?"

"I crochet dog sweaters," I said.

"Well, sure," she said with a smile. "That's kind of

"Will you be okay out here?" Suddenly I felt as if I was failing at everything I'd come out here to do. So far I had not run the inn even a little bit, since we'd had no guests, and Diantha seemed not to be taking well to my guardianship.

"Dahlia," Amal said, reaching a hand out but then seeming to think better of touching me. Probably something else Daisy had told her about me. "You're doing fine. It will take a while for her to get used to all the changes. And for you to settle in. This is new to both of you. But I'll be here. We don't have guests checking in until tomorrow afternoon," she reminded me. "And I'm making a spreadsheet of all the tasks involved with check in, so you'll be ready."

A spreadsheet. Perfect. I loved the idea of seeing all my responsibilities laid out in organized lines where I could easily keep track of what was expected of me. "Thank you, that's great." I turned to head into the apartment but then thought of something else. "And Amal? Thanks for helping with Diantha too. I think you know that part is harder for me."

"You'll be great."

"I'm going to bake," I told her, and turned to head through the big door.

The thumping music was louder than ever on the other side of my niece's door, and Taco was curled up outside it like he was guarding Diantha.

"Good boy," I told him. Taco often understood people a little better than I did.

I headed into the kitchen. If my niece needed a snack, that was something I was more than prepared to provide.

Daisy and I had grown up with the same grandmother, so I wasn't surprised to find a well-stocked pantry for baking. I took out shortening, flour, oatmeal, brown sugar, white sugar, and chocolate chips, and then dug in the refrigerator for eggs.

Soon, I was in a rhythm, beating shortening and sugars happily while gazing out the window over the kitchen counter, which looked down the hill toward the ocean. There were a few cottages below us, but the inn was situated to give the kitchen a view of the Pacific, moody under a blue-gray sky with craggy cliffs rising out of it on the sides of the bay.

Baking helped me click back into place. It was my happy pursuit when I felt like life was getting away from me. I controlled every element of a bake, and I could predict exactly how things would behave, given exact proportions and temperature.

I added the eggs and vanilla, preferring to beat it all by hand as my grandmother had taught us, even though there was a good stand mixer on the end of the counter. I'd use that for other things. Flour, salt and baking soda came next, and then the oatmeal, and finally a healthy amount of chocolate chips. Grandmother had added nuts for Daisy, but obviously, that wasn't an option with my allergies to worry about.

Next, I rolled the dough into logs wrapped in waxed paper and popped them into the refrigerator. I washed my hands and then tiptoed back around the corner to hear that the music had decreased in volume, and Taco was nowhere to be seen. I checked the other rooms, and then realized—my niece had let him into her room.

A strange feeling washed through me, and I stood still for a moment with my eyes closed, analyzing. I was happy Taco could comfort my niece since I wasn't sure if I could. But did I also feel just the tiniest bit... jealous?

That was silly. Diantha was a child. If Taco could be a friend to her, just as he was to me, then there was more than enough of his affection to go around. I could be without him for an hour.

Despite the fact I didn't think I had been since I'd gotten him.

I chilled the dough for a half hour, and then sliced the cookies, dropped them onto the cookie sheet I'd found in the cabinet, and slid them into the oven.

Just a few minutes into baking, the glorious smell of sugar and chocolate was wafting through the kitchen, and a few minutes later I was pulling one sheet out and putting a second in. That was about when Diantha and Taco appeared in the doorway.

"You made cookies?"

"I did," I said, turning to smile at my niece. "Would you like some?"

"Yes, please."

I waved her to a seat and soon we were both seated with cookies and milk in front of us.

It felt like progress.

Chapter Five

When Diantha headed off to school in the morning, I took Taco out for an early walk. We wandered up Nutmeg, the Main Street of town, and I realized only as we approached that I'd been steering us toward the Cliffside Restaurant.

It was early, and there was no one eating at the Cliffside when Taco and I arrived. There was also a sign on the window that notified diners that the restaurant would be closed for a day or two. I stood, gazing through the big plate glass window a moment, envisioning the loud man who'd garnered all the attention as he'd praised the swordfish special as though it was the best thing he'd ever tasted.

As I was about to turn away, wondering what I'd thought I'd find coming here, the front door opened and a round-faced man stepped toward me.

"Madame, we are closed for the foreseeable future due to unfortunate circumstances."

"Oh, well. Yes, that makes sense." I looked over the man who stood before me in his plastic clogs and white denim pants, a jaunty neckerchief tied around his neck. I wondered if I should give him my condolences or something, but as usual, I was at a loss for the most acceptable social reaction to a situation like this. And I wasn't totally sure who he was.

"Your dog is quite regal," he said, glancing down to where Taco sat at my side. Regal was not a word I would regularly apply to my service dog and friend, but at the moment, he was sitting tall, his excessive ruff puffed forward. He had a serious look on his face, and his square head was held high and proud. He did look regal.

"Well, thank you," I said on Taco's behalf. My dog promptly defeated any notions of being regal by letting his tongue loll out of one side of his mouth.

"The dog, he was here for lunch Tuesday?"

"Yes," I told him. "He's an allergen dog. We met with my attorney here for lunch."

"Oui. I remember. I am Chef Emile Teratine."

The chef waited expectantly for some sort of response, but I found nothing striking to add. "Hello," I managed.

"You did not have the swordfish?" he asked this, not meeting my eye.

"No, I didn't. My meal was perfect."

His chin came back up. "I am glad to hear it. So embarrassing, this situation. And now the police are coming to investigate, and the entire thing has been blown out of proportion, all thanks to one tiny error."

"An error?" I asked. I filed away the part about the police. Why would the police be investigating food poisoning?

"Oui. My sous chef — *embetante* — cannot tell the difference between herbs and deadly poison, evidently." The chef was rolling his eyes and gazing down Nutmeg Street to where the horizon was a line of perfect blue between the arching green of the trees as the Pacific met the grey sky of the afternoon.

"What do you mean?" I asked him, picturing the back tables strewn with herbs and rat poison side by side. Surely not.

"We forage," the chef said simply. "It is part of what makes the Cliffside special. Local ingredients, farm to table, field to table. But Adam went out to forage, and brought back what he thought was wild onion. But it was not. Any imbecile could tell the difference, even just from the smell alone."

"And you didn't notice either?" I asked. I'd seen enough cooking shows to know that chefs were very careful about what they let leave their kitchens.

Chef Teratine glared at me, his grey mustache twitching. "I was... there was something else requiring my attention."

"Oh, well that makes sense," I said, wondering what was more important than the food he was serving. It was his job, after all.

"Chef, here you are," a male voice came over my shoulder, and I turned to see a tall man in a button-down shirt and dark jeans approaching. His shirt was rolled up his forearms, and his square jaw and tousled sandy hair made him look like some kind of All American sports star.

"Oui," the chef said stiffly.

"Hello," said the man, who I noticed wore a badge at his belt.

"Hello," I echoed, lifting my gaze to find crystal green eyes staring back at me. How many people had truly green eyes?

"And who is this?" the man asked, holding out a hand to Taco who nuzzled it eagerly. An odd pang of something unfamiliar shot through me as the man turned his attention to my dog.

"Taco," I mumbled.

He grinned, and he might as well have smacked me, for the force with which his perfect smile hit me. "Taco, huh? Well, he's a beauty."

"Thank you," I said.

"I'm detective Sanderson," he told me, holding out a sturdy hand. "You can call me Owen."

"Oh." I shook his hand as the chef continued to stand, looking on.

"Most folks tell me their name at this point in the exchange," Owen said with a laugh.

"Right. I'm Dahlia Vale. Daisy Vale owned the Saltcliff Inn and I am her sister." Owen said nothing, and my mouth evidently thought it best to continue. "When she died, I was notified that I'd need to come take over operations and guardianship of my niece Diantha." The words spewed out of me as if I was under oath.

"He is not interrogating you," the chef muttered scornfully.

"Right," I said, feeling my cheeks flush. "Sorry."

"Great to meet you, Dahlia. And you too, Taco." Owen flashed that smile again, making it impossible for me to reply. "Also, I'm really sorry to hear of your sister's passing." And then he turned to Chef Teratine. "Could we go inside to talk?" he asked him.

"Oui," said the chef. The word was short and choppy, and I wondered why he was so annoyed about having to speak to the police. Was it just the interruption of his usual routine? Or something more?

Taco and I headed back to the inn, my mind whirling over what I'd learned.

Amal was waiting when we stepped inside.

"Good walk?" she asked.

"Interesting," I said, letting Taco off his leash. He

trotted over to drink noisily from his water dish while I thought about what the chef had said. "I met the chef from the Cliffside."

"Oh," Amal said, waiting as if she knew there would be more.

"Yes, it seems the poisoning was due to the accidental substitution of some naturally occurring poisonous plant for wild onion. The sous chef didn't know the difference."

Amal's dark eyebrow shot up. "Death Camas," she said simply.

"I'm sorry?"

She turned to the bookshelf behind the desk and pulled a worn scrapbook from it. She opened the book on the desk and began flipping through the pages.

"Your sister kept detailed notes of all the things she planted or allowed to grow in the garden out front. She spent years trying to banish the camas, which is essentially a weed, and finally just let it grow. She made a point of showing it to anyone who worked here and explaining just how toxic it is." Amal flipped to a page with a cut out image of a plant pasted in. The plant had tiny white flowers and long delicate green stalks that did look just like green onion. Another picture showed a bulb that certainly looked onion-like.

"The chef said it doesn't smell like onion."

"True, it doesn't."

"So wouldn't a trained sous chef realize that?"

Amal held my gaze for a moment and shook her head. "I have no idea. Seems like he would. The whole staff there is fairly new though, since the place just opened."

"New to the Cliffside, but surely not new to cooking?"

Amal shrugged and replaced the book where she'd gotten it, then turned her attention back to the computer on the registration desk.

With no real direction, I decided to do a little digging, purely to satisfy my own curiosity.

I opened my laptop on the coffee table in the lobby. I thought for a moment about my conversation with Chef Teratine and found a few news articles about the opening of the Cliffside, along with the early unfavorable review that had been excerpted by the article we'd read this morning, written by someone named Sally Trenton.

The first article I read raved about Chef Teratine's qualifications and gave a brief view into his background. He was married, I saw, and had moved to Saltcliff with his wife years ago after leaving a previous restaurant in Seattle. He'd run a restaurant in Monterey in the intervening years, and the Cliffside had opened less than a year ago.

The next piece provided a rundown of the staff—this seemed like something only a small-town paper with little competition for reporting space might include. It gave a headshot and brief bio for each of the staff members, including the less-than-friendly host I'd met. His name was Zane Thomas, and he was from the Bay area. The sous chef who'd been maligned in my earlier conversation was Adam Montrose, and this was actually his first position of responsibility in a kitchen. He'd served various positions in the front of house before, but the rest of his bio listed various businesses I'd never heard of. There were a few more photos and biographies of servers and bartenders, and a final photo that got my attention. John Baldwicki—the man who'd died from food poisoning at the restaurant. He was a partial owner.

Another article discussed the development project to take place just south of Saltcliff, where a large swath of open land was potentially being sold—by Baldwicki—to a hotel conglomerate with plans to turn it into a luxury resort. The effort was tied up in court, evidently, blocked by a group called Coastal Conservationists. Their spokesperson, who did not have nice things to say about the project was named Lana Lake. Fitting.

"Could be an adult film star," I muttered to myself. That'd be a tough name to grow up with, I figured. My grudge against my parents for naming me Dahlia lessened only slightly.

I pulled up one more page. The Saltcliff on the Sea Police Department. In its staff pages I found a photo of Detective Sanderson. The green eyes were almost as striking in his photograph as they had been in person, something I assured myself was merely an objective observation of fact. Nothing more.

Chapter Six

Amal was as good as her word. She presented me with a spreadsheet first thing the following morning, showing me every element of the guest check-in procedure, and she'd even created a second sheet called "during the stay" and a final one called "check out."

"Should I be embarrassed that this is exactly what I need?" I asked, realizing not everyone felt their entire world align perfectly when they had the ability to track things and check them off in perfect rows. But that was how it worked for me.

"Not at all. We all develop coping mechanisms to navigate life, and if they happen to be wildly helpful in terms of organization, then there's certainly no harm done." Amal smiled, and I realized how lucky I was that she was here.

"Thank you," I said, expressing my gratitude for the woman I barely knew.

"It will be a vast improvement over Daisy's methods, trust me." Amal chuckled sadly.

"You and my sister were close?" It seemed like Amal had to have been more than just an employee. But my instincts were rarely perfect in these situations.

Amal's eyes flicked to mine and then dropped, and for the first time I'd seen, she fidgeted, dropping the always elegant affect for a split second. She cleared her throat. "We were, yes."

"And how did she handle check in?" I asked.

Amal smiled now. "Mostly on the fly. She spent so much time out in the garden that sometimes she didn't even notice guests arriving. She'd come in to find them milling around wondering what they were supposed to be doing."

"Well that doesn't sound very welcoming," I said.

Amal's smile grew smaller. "She made up for it by being very charming."

I nodded. I did not have that particular skill set. "Well, thanks to your list, I will hopefully be right here when the first guests arrive this afternoon, ready with tea and cookies."

"They'll love that," she assured me.

I headed back into the apartment to check on Diantha's preparations for school. I found her in the kitchen, Taco right at her side as she shoveled cereal into her darkly glossed lips.

"Just about ready then?" I asked, hoping she was starting to adapt to her new routine—with me here instead of Daisy.

"I mwiirr ruuuurh nonnonnna."

Taco tilted his head and I frowned at my niece. "Maybe try again after you swallow."

She swallowed and wiped her mouth with the back of her hand, giving me a grin. "Sorry. I said I will be in a second."

"And everything at school..."

She took one last bite, chewed, and got up to carry the bowl to the sink, looking back over her shoulder at me. "Yeah, sorry about being rude yesterday, Aunt Dahlia. Sometimes I just get sad. I miss my mom." She looked down into the sink for a long moment while Taco pressed himself against her legs.

"I understand," I told her, wishing I had other words. More words. Better ones. "It hurts. And it will for a long time, but it will change over time. It will get easier."

Diantha turned to look at me. "Is that how it was with your mom?"

I shrugged. "We were very little when our mom died. But that was how it felt with Grandmother. Hard, and then easier."

"And do you miss my mom?"

I sighed. I knew the answer my niece wanted, knew she wanted to hear that my sister and I still shared some kind of bond. "I do, in a lot of ways. I miss the possibility that we might ever be friends again."

"She missed you all the time," Diantha said, and I felt her words in my chest. Daisy had a funny way of showing it.

"Well," I said, once again lost for words. "Better get to school, I guess." It was strange to think my sister had missed me at all. Hadn't she been the one to pull away?

"Guests coming today?"

"That's what Amal says, yes."

"Good. This place is too big for just us and Mr. Brown."

"Who?"

"He's the guest who never leaves." Diantha grinned, her dark eyes glinting with mischief. "A ghost, Aunt Dolly."

I opened my mouth to correct Diantha's use of my name, but stopped myself. I actually liked the nickname coming from her. It felt... tender.

"A ghost?" I laughed.

She shrugged and pulled her school bag up onto her shoulder, turning to head out to the lobby.

I wasn't sure about ghosts, but she was right about the other part. All those empty rooms upstairs. It would be nice to have them occupied. Plus, there was the simple fact that I would need to make some kind of income if I was going to support myself and my niece.

Diantha's departure left my morning free, and I was about to take Taco out for a walk, when Amal knocked at the apartment door.

I pulled it open, surprised to find her pale and worried looking. "You're not going to believe this," she said.

Taco and I went out into the lobby and looked at the computer screen where Amal had been scanning the news for the day.

"Local Businessman's Poisoning Being Investigated as Potential Homicide!" The article that followed noted that while other diners at the Cliffside had been poisoned with Death Camas, as the chef had told me, John Baldwicki's autopsy had turned up traces of another poison in his system.

"Someone killed him on purpose," Amal said, her eyes very wide.

"Would someone really do that?" I asked, but the answers were already percolating in my mind. Mr. Baldwicki had his fingers in several pots around town, and his plan to develop the marshlands certainly hadn't been popular. But was it a motive for murder?

My brain ticked into gear as I wondered, the parts of it that thrived on puzzles relishing the questions.

"There were many opponents to his development plans," I said.

"That's definitely true," Amal agreed. "But if anyone had a reason to kill him, it was probably Chef Teratine."

"What? Why?"

Amal's hands fumbled together, one turning a gold ring round and round on a finger of the other. "I didn't think there was a reason to spread gossip before so I didn't mention it to you, but it was fairly well known that Madame Teratine was having an affair with Mr. Baldwicki."

Surprise washed through me. "Oh. Well, yes. That would certainly annoy the chef."

Amal chuckled. "Yes, I think it really would."

I thought a little about that. I hadn't had many serious relationships in my life. Actually, I'd had only a few serious dates, really. But I couldn't imagine promising to spend your life with someone and then changing your mind without explicitly letting them know. Another reason I found people very confusing sometimes.

Taco still needed his morning walk, and I wanted the clear air to help me think a bit about everything that had happened since I'd arrived in Saltcliff. I'd anticipated a lot of changes—I hadn't expected a murder!

My other ulterior motive this morning was to check out the bakery I'd seen on the far corner of Nutmeg and Ginger. I loved eyeing other baker's creations for inspiration. And if we had guests arriving this afternoon, they'd be looking for breakfast treats tomorrow morning and sweets upon arrival.

"Let's go out, Taco," I called, and Taco practically slid across the lobby from down the hall where he'd been nosing about. He was so excited to go out that it was difficult to get his leash attached, but once I did, he settled down.

"He's cute," Amal said, smiling at us both.

"He is," I agreed. "And he's a good friend."

Taco let out a low groan of agreement. Or maybe he was simply reminding me that we were supposed to be going out.

Today we headed out through the inn's gardens and turned left instead of right. "We'll wander the rest of town a bit and come back via the main street," I told Taco.

He did not weigh in on my navigational plans other than to tug slightly at his leash.

Just to our left was an adorable cream-colored cottage with a roof shingled in the same curved shingles the inn had. The whole town looked like it had sprung right out of a book of fairytales. The other side of the street was made up of art galleries, bookstores, women's' fashion boutiques, and skincare stores. As we turned inland, we headed up Clove Street, which held many of the same kinds of stores. Sprinkled among the shops were hidden walkways that Taco and I investigated. Some led back to patios behind the stores, a few hid yet more stores, which I figured must be popular enough that being easily discoverable wasn't important. As Taco and I walked and explored, it was as if each corner held a new surprise—flowers bursting from a windowsill or an arched doorway leading into a used bookshop that smelled of coffee and worn pages.

No wonder Daisy had chosen this place to live. It was like inhabiting a story book all the time!

"We're definitely not in Kansas anymore, Taco," I said as we turned another corner and all but stumbled into a table set out on the sidewalk where two people sat, having coffee.

"Hello again." Detective Sanderson sat at the table with a mug nestled between his big hands. He looked perfectly at ease, despite the fact I'd nearly tripped directly into his lap. "Nope, this definitely isn't Kansas," he said. "Is that where you're from, Dahlia?"

I was flustered from having nearly fallen and from coming face to face—or really, it was more waist to face, since I was standing and he was not—with the detective so unexpectedly.

"No. Virginia," I told him, adjusting my sunglasses.

He smiled and lifted a hand to the dark-haired man at his side. He wore black framed plastic glasses and a white shirt that poofed up at the shoulders. Like a pirate, I thought.

"This is Duke Tippen. He is the chef at the Captain's Table. You'll have to try it next."

Aha, that was why his name was familiar. Diantha had told me about him when we'd gone to eat at the Cliffside.

"Nice to meet you. Dahlia Vale," I said. "And this is Taco." Taco bounced his head a bit as if agreeing with me.

"Hello," Duke said. Then he turned back to the detective. "I really do need to run, Detective. If there's nothing else?"

"Nope, I think I've got what I need." Detective Sanderson stood as the chef departed hurriedly. "Care to sit for a moment?" The detective indicated the vacated chair.

"Uh." This. This was when I disliked my squirrelly brain. I should have a simple "yes" ready to go, but instead, I was too busy thinking to form a proper answer.

Taco laid down as if he'd already decided to stay, and I slid into the chair, feeling the heat in my cheeks and wishing it would go away.

"How are you settling into Saltcliff?" Detective Sanderson asked.

"Well, thank you. I'm actually finding it very charming."

"Except for the murder and whatnot."

I met the detective's eyes, startled that he would just throw that out there. The green orbs shone and little wrinkles appeared around the corners, his dark lashes framing his gaze perfectly. He was most likely joking. But about murder?

"I'm kidding, Dahlia."

"But... I read the news. You do think it was murder?"

He nodded his head, causing a lock of sandy hair to fall across his tanned forehead. "Very likely, yes."

"Poison, you think? So something put on his food that day at the restaurant? You're probably considering the staff at the restaurant, then."

He smiled. "Are you playing a bit of detective, Ms. Vale?"

Maybe I had been, but of course it was silly to think I would have any intuition about this when I had none to offer about anything else. Only, wasn't a crime essentially a puzzle? Still, the detective had no reason to trust me or look to me for help.

"Do you suspect Chef Tippen?" I asked. He didn't have to answer if he didn't want to, I decided. "Ruining your competition's business would certainly help your own."

"That's true," he said. "But right now I'm just talking to everyone who might have ideas about what went on at the Cliffside that day." Detective Sanderson's gaze turned flinty. "You were there. Did you notice anything unusual?"

I told the detective about our meal, perhaps in more detail than he wanted.

"Anything else you picked up on while you were there? I'm getting the impression that you're a stickler for detail. Perceptive." He smiled, and a warm flush lit my chest. If I had good qualities, those were the ones. It was flattering to believe he'd noticed.

"Mr. Baldwicki made a call—or maybe answered one—while he was in the bathroom," I told him.

"You were in the bathroom with the victim?" The detective leaned forward and raised an eyebrow.

"The bathrooms are side by side, and the wall between them is quite thin, I think."

"What did you hear, Dahlia?" Now he looked amused.

"Mr. Baldwicki told someone that he was buying out the restaurant and that the frog was only the cook."

"I see." Detective Sanderson whipped out his phone and appeared to make a note. "Did he mention who he was speaking to?"

I shook my head.

"And your dining partner, Mr. Franklin, was it?"

"Yes."

"He was sickened as well. Did he notice anything while he was eating?"

"Not that he mentioned," I said. "But we ended up

sitting for quite some time, and by the time we left, he did look a little green."

The detective nodded. "Yes, that was pretty typical for the others. They all got sick hours after eating the swordfish, but most were feeling better by the morning. All except Mr. Baldwicki, of course."

"Who died," I said.

Detective Sanderson flashed his white-toothed smile again. "Right."

"Sorry. No need to restate the obvious." Why, oh why was I this awkward?

"Never hurts to be sure you're on the same page," Detective Sanderson said. "I, for one, prefer over-communicating to having to constantly try to figure out what people are thinking or feeling."

I peered at him, trying to decide if this was said as an acknowledgement of my own limitations or if it was the truth. Either way, I decided it was kind of him to say. "Yes."

We sat for a quiet moment, the cool springtime air breezing between us on its way down the colorful street.

"What happens next?" I asked. "In your investigation?"

Owen Sanderson leaned in a bit, one side of his mouth lifting in a half-smile. "Are you gunning for my job, Miss Vale?"

What? Why would he think that? "I... no, of course not."

The detective smiled wider. "It was a joke," he said, his tone reassuring.

"Of course." I dropped his gaze, tracing a bit of peeling paint on the tabletop with my fingertip. "Sometimes I take things very literally, sorry. It takes me a minute to realize when someone is kidding."

I risked a glance back up into those bright green eyes, and found them gazing steadily back at me. "I understand."

The words were simple, and something in me felt as if he really did. And there was a wealth of reassurance in that idea. Very few people did understand.

"Well, I don't normally discuss active investigations..."

I was about to stand, but the detective went on.

"The thing is... it would be easy for Chef Teratine to poison someone, but for his food to kill someone..."

"It wouldn't really help his reputation or his business," I said.

"Correct. Now, I could see his competition, as you said, wanting to strike a blow to his livelihood and reputation."

"So perhaps it was Chef Tippen?"

"Who was out of town on a two-week cruise until this morning."

I nodded. Chef Tippen probably couldn't be the killer, then. "Plus, why would he randomly select one person to harm? It would make more sense to poison several people if he wanted to raise issues about the quality of his competition's food."

"I agree. Though technically, that is what happened."

"True, but Chef Teratine said that the food poisoning was a mistake made by the sous chef. So whoever the real killer was, they had an issue directly with Mr. Baldwicki."

"I think so."

"Who else is there?" I asked, but the detective's open gaze told me he was more willing to let me figure things out than he was to share actual investigative information with me. "Was Mr. Baldwicki married?"

"Never."

"And did he have business partners?"

"In the restaurant, yes, but not in this particular venture. Others, in the past, I believe."

I nodded. "The health food business."

The detective smiled. "You've been very busy, Miss Vale."

"What about the Chef himself? I heard a rumor that his wife and the victim..."

Detective Sanderson sighed and leaned back in his chair. "Yeah. You know, sometimes this job really challenges my faith in people."

"I can understand that," I said, thinking about all the

things he must learn about people in this line of work. "But most people are inherently good, don't you think?"

"Are they?" The detective's handsome face took on an expression I thought was probably wry. A smile, but not a happy one.

"I like to think so," I told him.

"Well, I like that idea." He finished the last of his coffee and put the cup down, then leaned down to give Taco a few belly rubs. My dog, who had no shame at all, rolled farther onto his back, lifting a back leg into the air and bracing it on the detective's chair as he groaned in delight.

After a moment, Detective Sanderson rose. "Well, thanks for the chat. Hopefully we'll see each other again soon."

I rose as well, and Taco took the cue to get back to his feet. "Yes," I said. "I mean, okay. Sure."

The detective smiled. "If you learn anything interesting in your investigations, I hope you'll share it."

"I'm not a detective, Detective," I said, but the detective didn't look annoyed or angry.

"Maybe not, but you are observant and smart, Miss Vale. Let me know if you pick anything up. And please call me Owen."

"I will." I watched as Owen stepped out into the late morning sunlight and made his way down the street.

I liked the detective, and the idea that I'd made a friend already gave me a bit of a confidence boost.

"Come on, Taco. We need to scope out the bakery for ideas."

Chapter Seven

Beachside Bakery was an adorable glass-fronted shop situated on a corner at Nutmeg and Ginger, and as soon as I pulled the door open, the scents of vanilla, cinnamon, and sugar wrapped me in a familiar hug.

"Hello there!" called the red-headed woman behind the counter. I gave her a smile as I approached, envying the easy glamor she managed with all that wavy red hair wound up in some kind of updo that looked casual but was probably very complicated to achieve. Way beyond my feminine skill set, at least.

"Hello," I said, my eyes drawn to the glass case beneath the counter. It was lit with soft yellow light, which perfectly illuminated tiny fruit tarts, mini cheesecakes topped with strawberries and decorative candied lemon wedges, muffins, slices of fancy breads, and a variety of macarons and croissants. "Wow, what a selection."

I glanced back up at the woman, and her easy smile widened. "It is. Take your time."

"Oh, I wasn't going to choose anything. I'm just here to get ideas."

"I see." The woman crossed her arms, the smile dropping a bit, and I realized I'd said the wrong thing.

"Erm, I mean, not to steal your recipes or anything. I'm a baker too."

The eyes narrowed. This was not getting better.

"I'm Dahlia Vale? My sister was Daisy Vale." Maybe I could reverse this situation by borrowing some of Daisy's charm.

The woman's gaze softened. "Poor Daisy," she said, dropping her arms. "I'm so sorry for your loss. It's nice to meet you, though. I'm Valerie Killeen."

"A pleasure to meet you," I said. "I fear I'm not presenting my intentions well."

Valerie laughed. "Well, so far I've gathered that you're not going to buy anything and that you're planning to open a rival bakery and put me out of business."

I lifted my hands in front of me. "Oh no, not at all!" Taco whined at my side, as if disappointed again at how I'd managed to mangle another simple interaction. "I'm taking over the inn until my niece is twenty-two. And I bake when I'm stressed."

Valerie's nose wrinkled and she laughed again. "Well that explains everything."

"Does it?" I asked.

"No, not really," she said.

"I'm sorry. Let me try. I have always baked. Mostly for myself, but since I have always lived alone, that meant taking a lot of things to work for other people to enjoy. I understand an expectation at the inn is that there will be baked goods available at check in, at tea time, and at breakfast, so I am well equipped to handle this responsibility. But I am from the East Coast, and just wanted to see what kinds of expectations visitors to Saltcliff might have as far as pastry."

Valerie's easy smile returned. "I have always thought that the language of butter, flour, and sugar was pretty universal."

"You may be right." I looked longingly at a lemon tart in the case. "And actually, I will buy something if you don't mind."

"Mind? It's kind of why I'm here, Dahlia."

"Right." I felt the familiar flush rush up my cheeks. "May I have a lemon tart, please? And a cup of Earl Gray?"

"Of course," Valerie said. "Would your pup like a biscuit? You'll find that most of the stores in Saltcliff cater almost as much to dogs as we do to their owners."

I glanced down at Taco who seemed to be telling me that the answer was obviously yes as two strands of drool hung from his jowls. Even the potential that someone might feed him set him to drooling. It was embarrassing sometimes.

"He would like that, thank you."

Valerie handed me the tart on a little plate with a bone-shaped biscuit next to it, and a cup of hot water and a tea bag. I thanked her and paid, and Taco and I went out to the sidewalk to sit and watch the business of the day unfold along Saltcliff's main street.

There was a table at my side, where two well-dressed women were deep in conversation, each of them leaning over their elbows as they discussed something that held their attention firmly.

I steeped my tea and sat, enjoying the sun and breeze, and not intending to eavesdrop. But the women were so engrossed, they didn't seem to notice me there. And they weren't exactly quiet. I gave Taco his cookie and spread my napkin across my lap.

"I'm just saying, Antoinette does not seem especially sad about the whole thing. Maybe she didn't even love him."

The second woman laughed, but it didn't sound like she actually found the statement amusing. "How would she mourn without admitting she was sleeping with him? Her husband wouldn't be very sympathetic, I don't think. Plus, since when do you have to be in love with someone to be sleeping with them?"

"Right. But honestly, it's not as if the whole town didn't already know," the first woman said.

"Do you think she killed him?" The other woman asked in a loud whisper. "I heard he ended things."

Now I couldn't pull my attention away if I wanted to. I took a little bite of the lemon tart, and the creamy lemon flavor flooded my tongue. Sweet and tart all at once. Perfection.

"I'm surprised her family wants anything to do with her," the first woman was saying. "It seems like she's slept with half the men in town. It's got to be humiliating for Nadine and for Emile."

"At least most of the men she sleeps with don't end up dead."

I couldn't help turning my head to look at the women more closely. They both glanced over at me and I busied myself with my teabag. They were talking about Mr. Baldwicki. Antoinette must be Chef Teratine's wife.

The women shifted subjects after that, and I lost interest in their chat about the upcoming theater production of *A Streetcar Named Desire*. My mind was too busy turning over the possibility that Baldwicki had recently ended his affair with the chef's wife.

Even though I wanted to see if I could go find the detective again to share this information, I needed to get back to the inn and begin getting ready for check in. I dropped into Brunelli's Market on the way home and picked up some fresh lemons and eggs, and twisted off a few sprigs of rosemary in Daisy's garden on the way in.

I wasn't going to steal Valerie's recipe, just the inspiration I'd taken from it.

Lemon tarts were on my mind—it had taken a lot of willpower not to go back in and order a second one, but I knew my waistline didn't need the challenge. Since I'd leaped over the chronological dividing line between my thirties and forties, it seemed that calories were easy enough to put in, but they didn't seem to leave in quite the same way they once had.

I did bake lemon tarts, infusing them with the rosemary I'd picked and setting the tray into the refrigerator to chill. Those would be lovely to present tomorrow, I figured. But for check in today, I needed something a bit less time intensive. Lemon curd was quick enough to whip up, and while it cooled, I threw together a simple white cake batter, zesting another lemon to give the fluffy white crumb a tiny little zing. The magic, however, was in the filling, and when the layers had cooled, I spread cream cheese frosting generously over the first layer, piping an edge so I could fill it with lemon curd. Then I carefully set the second layer on top, frosted the entire thing and filled the top with another layer of lemon curd, finishing the whole thing with carefully piped starflowers all around the top edge.

Perfect. A little glow of pride washed through me as I

cleaned up the cake plate, shooing Taco away from the counter for the three thousandth time.

"How can you be so well trained when it comes to legumes, but I haven't been able to teach you to lie down and stay when I'm working in the kitchen?" I frowned at my big brown dog, but as usual, I found it very difficult to actually be angry with him. He was underfoot. It was part of his charm.

"Let's take this out to the lobby," I said, and Taco danced from one foot to the other as if I'd just announced that the whole cake was actually for him.

Used to disappointment where food was concerned, Taco watched me carry the cake out to the front and set it on the side table near the registration desk where a tea set, coffee urn, and several small plates and cutlery were already arranged.

"Dahlia, that is beautiful," Amal said, stepping close to peer down at the cake.

I turned to her, happy to hear that I'd succeeded at my first task of inn keeping. "Would you like a piece?" I asked.

The elegant woman smiled, her eyes glowing as they met mine. "Normally, I would decline, but I do find that people are more likely to partake if it appears someone else already has," she said.

That was true. People were reluctant to be the first to cut into a pristine cake. "You're right."

"So I will have a bit, but only for the good of all."

I glanced over my shoulder at her again, certain she did not believe that eating cake would in any way benefit the human population. Her gentle smile assured me she was joking, and I did find the concept amusing. I chuckled as I handed her a plate and a fork, feeling more at ease than I had since arriving in Saltcliff.

"You're not having any?" she asked, as she settled on the couch in front of the gently glowing fireplace.

"I would, but I visited the Beachside Bakery and had a lemon tart earlier," I told her.

"You met Valerie," she said.

"I did."

"A great source of sugar and tea," she said, wiggling her eyebrows.

"I also had tea," I confirmed.

Amal chewed a bite with a thoughtful expression, and then explained. "Tea to drink, yes, but I meant gossip. Valerie always seems to know what is going on around town."

"Ah." I had heard that before, I realized. Spilling the tea. I would need to remember it. "Good to know."

"How are things going with Danny?" Amal asked, her voice taking a careful tone.

"Better, I think. She seems like a good girl."

"She is a good girl. Smart, curious. Funny." Amal's eyes glistened.

"You have spent a lot of time with her?" I asked.

Amal nodded, her face growing sad as she lowered her plate. "Dahlia, surely you've realized. Your sister and I..."

Amal didn't finish her sentence because at that moment, the front door swung open with a whoosh and the little bells over the door tinkled merrily as a man and a woman stepped in, each tugging a wheeled suitcase.

Taco pranced over to greet them, but I called him back. Some people were afraid of big dogs. He sat obediently at my side again, but he quivered with the desire to go make new friends.

"Hello!" Amal shot to her feet and turned to face them. "You must be the Robertsons."

"Last we checked," the man said, chuckling. He wore a Hawaiian shirt pulled tight across a very impressive gut, and had short grey hair cropped close around his smiling face. The woman at his side wore a loose-fitted dress in an identical Hawaiian print.

"I trust you found us all right?" Amal asked, stepping behind the registration desk. I moved to her side, ready to learn how to check in my first guests.

"Oh, sure," Mr. Roberston said. "The taxi driver knew exactly where to go when I said the Saltcliff Inn."

"What beautiful gardens you have out front," Mrs. Robertson commented.

"The original owner put her heart and soul into them," Amal said, and that statement sent Mrs. Robertson's smile my way.

Amal showed me how to pull up the correct reservation in the software and mark the couple as having arrived. We ensured the card on file was correct, and then assigned the Gatsby Suite to the Robertsons, one of the rooms on the top floor.

"There is a lovely lemon cake, as well as tea and coffee all ready for afternoon tea," Amal told them, indicating the side table. Taco had planted himself to one side of it, most likely hoping someone would swing by and accidentally tip the cake onto the floor for him.

"And a very big dog," Mrs. Robertson said, her voice going quite high.

Taco's ears perked. He knew she was talking to him.

"That is Taco," I said. "He is a service dog."

"May I pet him?" she asked, her gaze moving to mine. She had deep brown eyes, and something about them was reassuring. Friendly.

"Of course," I told her. "Thank you for asking."

Taco got to his feet as she approached, and nosed the hand she extended before pressing himself against her shins as she lavished pets and love on him.

"He's a darling," she said. "And this cake looks so luscious. Oh my."

"Let's get to the room. We can come back down for cake," Mr. Robertson said. "Thank you, ladies."

"Do you need any help with your luggage?" I asked.

"I think we've got it handled," Mr. Robertson said. "See you in a bit."

With that, the Robertsons headed off down the hallway Amal had pointed out, and we heard them climbing the stairs a moment later.

"Pretty easy?" she asked me.

"I think so." Amal made a little note on a pad behind the desk. "I learned something interesting today at the bakery," I told her.

She swallowed visibly and then her chin tilted up. "What was it?"

"Two women were talking about Chef Teratine's wife. Evidently she was involved romantically with other men before Mr. Baldwicki. And Baldwicki had recently ended things with her."

Amal's eyebrows shot up. Finally, something she didn't already know.

"You know, Daisy and Antoinette were good friends," Amal said.

It was my turn to frown. "They were?"

Amal lifted a shoulder and turned to walk back to the registration desk. "It's a very small town. In Saltcliff you know everyone, some better than others."

That did seem to be true.

"Do you know her very well? The chef's wife?"

Amal shook her head. "No. Her relationship with Daisy seemed to revolve around plants." She smiled, a half-smile that didn't quite reach her eyes. "That was strictly Daisy's domain."

I wondered if the chef's wife had as impressive a garden as my sister did, and made a note to see if Taco and I might walk past her house to find out.

My train of thought was interrupted by the next guests arriving.

Chapter Eight

By dinner time that evening, the little inn was almost full. All the suites except for the Emma were occupied and the very air inside the place felt cozier, closer. More like a home.

"I like it when there are people here," Diantha said over her plate of pasta as we sat at the little dining room table.

Amal sat at her side—I'd invited her to stay for dinner, and then she'd cooked it for us at Diantha's request. Evidently, Amal had spent more nights here than not when Daisy was alive, and her presence felt comfortable and right.

"How is school going, Danny?" Amal asked. "Is it hard being back?"

My niece lifted a narrow shoulder. "Everything is harder without Mom," she said softly. "But it feels better to be doing things. To be getting back to normal a little bit." Her big eyes squeezed shut for a moment. "I feel guilty saying that," she whispered.

Amal reached over to lay a hand on her shoulder and a twinge of envy shot through me that she understood so well how to soothe my niece. "That's completely normal, honey. But we both know that your mother wanted that for you. For us all. For life to go on."

Diantha nodded, and then her shoulders straightened and she took another big bite of pasta. "How waf fo thay?" she asked, looking over at me.

"Again?" I suggested.

She swallowed. "Sorry. How was your day? Getting the hang of everything?"

"I think that will take quite a while," I said. "I'm just glad you and Amal are here to keep things going while I learn."

We ate in silence for a few moments, and then Diantha said, "Have you solved the murder yet?"

I put my fork down. "I'm not in charge of solving the murder. That is Detective Sanderson's job."

Diantha smiled. "But you're working on it, aren't you?"

I thought about that. I had been very curious, and if I was honest with myself, I had been gathering some mental clues in the course of my day to day activities—not purposely, just picking up those that seemed to fall across my path. But was I actually trying to solve the case? "I guess I've been doing a bit of investigating."

"Mom always said there was no puzzle you couldn't solve, or that you'd drive everyone nuts trying to solve it." Diantha twirled another forkful of pasta and stuck it in her mouth.

"A particular talent of yours," Amal said, winking at me. "She envied it."

That got my attention. My sister had envied me? In the long years we'd been side by side, my perspective had been that she was the one with the enviable gifts.

But I did have a knack for puzzles. That was true.

"After dinner can I take Taco for a walk?" Diantha asked, her eyes wide and hopeful.

Taco, hearing his name and the word "walk," was already on his feet.

"I think he'd like that," I said.

When the dishes were cleared, all four of us headed back out to the lobby, where a couple of our guests were sitting quietly by the fire, reading.

Amal busied herself checking to see that the tea kettle was full and there was plenty of milk and sugar for the guests, and Diantha and I headed out for our walk with Taco.

"You lead the way," I suggested.

Diantha nodded, and guided us to the left several blocks before we headed up a treelined street populated by cottages with curving roofs and painted in pastel colors interspersed with more square Spanish-style homes that were no less quaint. A few had striped awnings, and each had at least a few flowering shrubs or mounds of blooms along the walkway.

"This place looks like the whole village was created just for a movie set," I said, partially to myself. I had never known such a place existed.

"It's a little extra," Diantha said.

"Extra what?"

"Just extra everything."

It was. But I loved it.

"The Teratines live in that one," Diantha said, pointing to a two-story Spanish-style house with a red tile roof. In front, there was a retaining wall and a walkway gated with a wrought iron fence in an intricate design. Just beyond the gate was a garden, bursting with greenery and blooming in every imaginable color.

"Mom was over here a lot when they moved here, helping with the garden," Diantha said, staring into the vibrant space wistfully. "And then she and Mrs. Teratine used to hang out and drink wine together."

"They did?" I asked, trying to picture sitting with Daisy, sipping a glass of wine and laughing. I wished we'd gotten to do that. "It's beautiful," I said.

"'Allo?" Just then a head popped up along the walkway, topped with a mass of blond curls and tied with a scarf, like a movie star. "Ah, Danny. How are you?" The woman stepped out so we could see her fully, one of her gloved hands holding a plant she must have been about to plant, its twisted roots looking withered and forlorn as they dangled from her hand. She wore a pair of bright orange, tightly fitting capri pants and a white blouse, tucked in at her slim waist, which emphasized the immense curve of her chest. Her voice was soft and she spoke with a vague accent, which I took to be French.

"Madame Teratine," Diantha said. "Hello."

The woman deposited the plant at the edge of the walkway and strode toward us, pulling her gloves from her long, elegant hands. "And you must be Daisy's sister," she said, addressing me.

"I am."

Madame Teratine reached her arms out for Diantha, who stepped in. I watched, mystified, as the woman planted an air kiss on either side of Diantha's head, and my niece did the same to her.

"So wonderful to meet you," Madame Teratine said, stepping close and repeating the same action with me. My body was jerky and awkward as I leaned in and air kissed this woman I'd never met.

"Please, call me Antoinette," the woman said, stepping back. "She was a wonderful woman, our Daisy. Very knowledgable about plants. And people." She winked at me as she said this last and then let out a light laugh. "We were good friends." She dropped my gaze as she said this, and I was struck by how many friends my sister had here, how many people her death affected.

"Thank you," I said, hoping that was the right response. "Your garden is lovely."

"Ah," she shrugged. "A little hobby. Nothing more. To pass the time while my husband is constantly working."

"Restaurants take a lot of focus, I guess."

"Oui." This was followed by a sniff. "And you ladies, what are you up to this evening while I am digging in the dirt?" She winked at us and put on a playful smile.

"Just walking Taco Dog," Diantha answered. "Aunt Dolly is still learning her way around town."

The woman gave me a bright smile then. "It is a lovely place. You will be happy here, I think," she said. "My best advice?" She put a hand to her chest and leaned forward, as if she was about to share a great secret. "Don't worry about what people say. As your sister would tell me, 'you do you.'"

"Mom did say that, didn't she?" Diantha asked, smiling at Madame Teratine.

"She said it, and she lived it. You remember that, little Danny." The woman gave Diantha's face a little caress, then looked to me. "You remember it too."

"Um, okay," I said. It felt a bit odd getting life advice from a woman who appeared to be my own age. Though she did have a certain worldly air about her as if she'd seen and done things far outside this little town.

"I'm going to have a little gathering soon, I think," she said. "You must come."

I stilled. Had I just been invited to a party? "A...a gathering?"

"Just some friends, some wine," she said, laughing at my sudden uncertainty. "Sunday, oui? Two o'clock. Amal too."

Diantha bounced a little on her toes. "And me?"

"Grown up ladies this time," Madame Teratine said.

Diantha let out a sigh, but said nothing else.

"Thank you," I told her, and Diantha and I wandered on down the sidewalk. In a strange way, it felt as if Daisy was here still, paving the way for me just like she had when we were young. I swallowed hard, trying not to think too much of the sister I'd lost.

"A party," Diantha said, a shade of envy making her voice lower. "See? You've already made friends here."

I let that sink in a bit and then smiled down at my niece. "You've helped a lot with that," I said. "You know, your mom did that too."

"Did what?" Diantha's eyes were wide as she looked up at me.

"She connected people; made it feel easy for me to make friends and be with people I would have been nervous around normally." It occurred to me that my niece might like to know the little bit I knew about her mother. I made a mental note to talk more about the sister I was missing more and more each day. "You're like her in that way," I told her. Diantha's face glowed as we rounded another corner and headed back to the inn.

Back at the inn, Diantha headed off to bed. I spent a few minutes tidying the lobby, and then went to the kitchen to prepare a few things to pop into the oven in the morning.

My brain worked through all the events of the past few days as I mixed and kneaded, Taco in a comforting dark brown pile nearby.

Finally, I brewed a cup of herbal tea and carried it to the back bedroom, still feeling a bit like an intruder in my sister's space.

I set the tea on the little round table that sat next to the single armchair next to the window and sat down, letting the weight of the day sink in as my eyes scanned my sister's things.

My suitcase still sat on the bench at the end of the bed, overflowing with clothes as I pulled things out and put them back in. I could, I supposed, have used a few drawers in the dresser, but the one I'd opened had been filled with socks. Daisy's socks. Something about the idea of removing her things to replace them with my own didn't feel right to me, so for now, I was at an impasse.

I sipped my tea, and did my best to sort through the information and feelings I'd been gathering since arriving here.

It was funny how easy it had been to leave one life and step into another. I'd lived on the East Coast for a full decade, not speaking to my sister once during that time. For most people, you'd assume abandoning a ten-year part of your life would result in some distress, or at least a few phone calls from those you'd left, people who missed you. But as I thought about the many people I'd met here in just a few short days and then sorted through those I'd known for years in Virginia, I realized that there was a vast difference. I was already certain that if I left Saltcliff suddenly, Amal would call me to make sure I was all right. I thought maybe even Tessa down the street or Detective Sanderson might wonder where I'd gone and reach out. I knew Diantha would worry.

And that was something.

To have forged a relationship with my niece so quickly... I knew I would never replace my sister. I wouldn't want to, of course. But getting to be with her daughter as she grew, to be trusted to take good care of her on my sister's behalf—it was a more binding relationship than any I'd had. Since Daisy and I were little.

The next morning, I rose before the sun to make scones, muffins, bacon and eggs for our guests.

Having tired myself of lemons the day before with the cake and the rosemary-lemon tart chilling in the refrigerator for this afternoon, I decided to stick to tradition, and made my favorite blueberry crumble muffins and orange blossom scones.

By seven-thirty, I had laid out the baked goods, setting the scrambled eggs and bacon in a metal pan with a warming candle beneath it to keep them warm. Guests were just beginning to arrive to eat when Diantha slouched out into the lobby looking sleepy beneath the thick eye makeup and took a muffin to the deep armchair near the fireplace.

Taco settled next to her as she slumped into a straight-backed chair near the reception desk where I stood. He watched her eat eagerly, clearly hoping for crumbs.

"What will you do today?" she asked.

I had been thinking about that very thing.

"I think I'll do some baking ahead for the week. There are a few doughs I can chill until it's time to bake them. And tomorrow is Sunday, so we'll need to get brunch planned and ready to prepare in the morning."

"What are you going to wear to the party?" Diantha asked, her eyebrows wiggling as she shoved half a muffin into her mouth. Taco dove for the crumbs that cascaded down her shirt to the floor.

I moved to the side table and picked up a plate, which I handed her. "I was just planning to wear... whatever I put on tomorrow." I hadn't thought about it. I tended to wear a uniform of sorts on days when I wasn't going into the office. Which was every day now.

My hands smoothed down the front of my dark, functional slacks, and I glanced down at the white tennis shoes I always wore to walk Taco. Today I'd pulled on a T-shirt that said "A well-read woman is a dangerous creature." I had a collection of shirts with literary sayings I found amusing. They'd previously been reserved for days at home with Taco, but now I figured every day was a day at home.

"Your shirts are fun," Diantha said, and I wasn't sure I liked the speculative way she was eyeing me now, as if I was a project, not a person. "But we need to do something about the rest."

"The rest? The rest of me?"

Diantha's big brown eyes found my face and softened. "Can I take you shopping, Aunt Dolly?"

I didn't have a ton of money to spare, and shopping had never been one of my favorite activities. My uncertainty must have shown on my face.

"Don't worry," Diantha said. "We won't even have to leave the inn."

Confusion wrinkled my brow and I shook my head lightly. "Is there a store here?"

"Kind of," Diantha said. "Meet me inside in an hour." My niece leapt off the armchair she'd occupied and dropped her plate into the little bin next to the side table where guests put dirty dishes, then she dashed inside the apartment, taking Taco with her.

"Well, okay," I said, mystified, but pleased to see my niece looking energized about something.

I spent the next hour with my laptop open at the big table in the lobby. It was Amal's day off, and while she'd made it clear I did not need to be available at all times, I felt some responsibility to the guests until they'd headed out for the day.

I'd had a particular subject in mind when I pulled up the internet browser: John Baldwicki.

Given that the man had seemed to enjoy the spotlight, there was plenty to be found. I began with the local high school, since Tessa Damlin had mentioned that they'd been in school together.

Saltcliff High, it turned out, graduated small classes. It was easy enough to find the yearbook, showing John Baldwicki in many of the photos. He was the treasurer of his class, and appeared to have been involved in a wide range of clubs and activities. In many of the photos, the same boy appeared at his side—a thin boy with a dark shock of hair hanging over his face. Adam Montrose, according to the captions. From what I could tell, they seemed to be good friends. The name was familiar too. The sous chef?

I couldn't find mentions of John for a couple years after graduation, but then he popped up in a small article describing a trading firm he was heading, helping seniors multiply their retirement savings. Another article, dated only two years later, described how the firm had imploded, leading many of its investors to lose money. Interestingly, Adam Montrose appeared in the articles too. He'd played some role in managing the firm with Baldwicki, apparently.

There were actually a few other businesses registered in Baldwicki's name when I did a search on the government site, nothing I could find much information for, so it appeared he'd had several failed ventures. One showed a sale, though—a company called Lean Green. That must have been the health food company with the green smoothies. He'd sold it for a substantial sum, according to coverage of the sale in a California business paper.

Lean Green hit the market just as the concept of the

"green drink" went viral across social media, the article explained. *Mr. Baldwicki capitalized on the concept by developing several versions of his company's green drink, and he himself launched a variety of social media accounts espousing the benefits of the drink. When a national beverage conglomerate decided to enter the space, acquiring Baldwicki's platform was a natural alternative to starting from scratch, making Baldwicki wealthy in the process.*

Mr. Baldwicki had gotten lucky at last, I guessed.

"Is there any more coffee?" Mr. Robertson asked, peering over the top of my laptop screen and startling me.

"Oh!" I slammed the lid shut and immediately felt the blush climb my cheeks. He certainly would think I'd been looking at something I shouldn't have been, based on my reaction and my brain raced to decide how to assure him I was not. "That wasn't porn," I heard myself say.

Oh, that wasn't the right thing.

Mr. Robertson's eyebrows shot up to his hairline, but then his whole face relaxed and he let out a deep laugh. "None of my business anyway, Ms. Vale. Just hoping for some caffeine is all."

"Of course," I stammered, rising and heading over to the sideboard to brew a fresh pot. "It'll just take a moment or two."

Mr. Robertson stood nearby as I made the pot, and when it was brewing away, he spoke again. "Do you have any suggestions for things we should see here in Saltcliff?"

he asked. "We're just sticking around here today to recover from the travel. We'll head out and see some of the area's attractions tomorrow."

"I do," I told him, moving to the registration desk to get the brochure my sister had created, showing the highlights of our little town. "I'm new here too, but my sister lived here a decade and used to run the inn. She had this to hand out to guests."

Mr. Robertson took the little brochure and thanked me, and then spent a bit of time reviewing it while he waited for the coffee. Soon, he'd taken two cups back to his room and I was alone again in the lobby.

I glanced at the big clock on the wall. It was time for me to see what my niece was planning for me inside.

Chapter Nine

Inside the apartment, I was greeted by Diantha wearing attire very different from her usual assortment of baggy, black draperies. The eye makeup was still firmly in place, as were the very dark lips, but now she wore a pink sheath sundress with a bright yellow belt, and a pair of low-heeled yellow sandals.

I did my best to stifle any reaction, sensing that expressing how lovely I thought she looked might send her running back for the fishnets slung over the desk chair just beyond the open door of her bedroom.

Taco sat at her side with a yellow bow tied around his neck.

They both looked quite pleased with themselves.

"Welcome," Diantha said. "To Danny's Boutique."

I felt my eyebrows go up as I gazed around the living room, which had been transformed to some degree.

There were dresses hanging in every possible place and draped over furniture. In place of the magazines that usually covered the coffee table were folded denim pants, and folded shirts covered the sofa and chairs. Blouses and skirts were draped over the dining table, and a surprisingly colorful assortment of shoes lined the far wall.

"What size shoe are you, Aunt Dolly?"

"I wear a seven," I said, still uncertain how to react. These had to be Daisy's things.

"Perfect!" Diantha clapped her hands excitedly, and then reached for my hand, leading me to the dining table.

"We're going to start with a look I like to call 'innkeeper chic.'"

"Um, okay," I said, imagining my sister wearing the simple green A-line skirt Diantha picked up to pair with a white blouse that had embroidered floral detailing along the neckline and sleeves with a little pouf at each shoulder.

"Go try this on," Diantha suggested.

I took the clothing from her hands and wandered to the bathroom, still sorting through my feelings. Would it be right to wear my sister's things? Would people think I was being too bold, trying to take her place? But her daughter was the one I'd worry most about in that department, and she was the one foisting Daisy's things into my hands.

I tucked in the white blouse and gazed at myself in the full-length mirror on the back of the door. The outfit was clean and simple, but stylish in a way I never managed to look.

"Let's see!" Diantha called from just beyond the door.

I pulled it open, and she gave me a broad grin. "Perfect!" She moved to the wall and picked out a pair of natural colored wedge sandals. "Put these on."

I followed directions and then stood before her, my heart doing something strange inside my chest.

"You should wear this when guests are checking in," she said. Her eyes dropped to the floor. "That's when Mom wore that outfit." She sniffed.

I was about to tell her we didn't have to do this, that it didn't feel right, but she brought her eyes back up to mine and the big smile reappeared. "Okay, now for something that says, 'I'm here to make friends.' Something you can wear to the party tomorrow."

We both wandered around the assortment of clothing draped everywhere. "This?" I asked, lifting the sleeve of a long-sleeved floral dress.

Diantha shook her head. "That says, 'I'm channeling Little House on the Prairie.' I've never liked that one."

"Oh, okay," I said, surprised she'd heard of Little House, but not surprised my taste ran in the modest, farm girl direction.

"This?" Diantha asked, holding up a purple sheath dress that had ruffles running over one of the shoulders and partway across the chest.

"I'm not going to be accepting an Academy Award," I laughed. "I think that's too much."

She smiled and put it back, pulling out a sundress with a full skirt and sunflower pattern on the fabric. "Better?"

"I could wear that," I said, taking it from her. "Maybe with a cardigan or something?"

Diantha nodded and disappeared into the back bedroom, returning with a white cardigan sweater. "Perfect."

We spent another couple hours putting together outfits I thought I would actually wear, mixing Daisy's things with my own until I had a new wardrobe that felt appropriate for the new life I'd adopted. As we sorted out the items I didn't think I'd ever wear into a separate pile, I took a moment to really look at my niece.

"Is this really okay with you?" I asked her, gesturing to the pile that we were clearly sorting to donate.

She turned to face me, and for a moment I thought she might cry. Her expression faltered and her bottom lip wobbled. She squeezed her eyes tightly, but then opened them wide and looked up at me. "It's hard," she said. "But seeing Mom's clothes will make it feel a little bit like she's still here. Plus, I think she'd like knowing you were wearing them." She ran a hand down an electric yellow skirt that had gone into the no way pile. "And she would definitely have agreed that you needed an upgrade."

I chuckled. "She would have." Daisy had been my

stylist for years when we'd lived in the same place, always assuring me that her taste was my taste—I just didn't know it. I'd been adrift in Virginia in more ways than one. Clearly, my fashion know-how had suffered as well.

"Do you want to keep these somewhere? Just in case?"

"In case of what?" Diantha asked.

I didn't have a good answer, and was shocked at how easily my niece said the words. "In case Mom comes back? Aunt Dolly, she's gone. She's not coming back."

I let my eyes slide shut as that truth worked through me. There was a box of ashes in the top of the closet in my room that agreed with Diantha's words. My sister was gone.

"Okay," I said softly, and without planning it, I reached for my niece, who stepped into the circle of my arms. For a long moment, we stood like that, comforting each other in the absence of the woman we both missed so much.

"Roowr," Taco groaned from where he lay sprawled in front of the apartment door.

Diantha laughed and broke away, going to scratch his belly. "You don't like being left out, do you?"

That night, we cleaned up the rest of the clothing, arranged my new wardrobe in the closet in my bedroom and stored my suitcase just inside the basement door in the kitchen. I also put a box of Daisy's things there. Maybe I was the one who wasn't ready to let them go quite yet.

"I don't like going down there," Diantha told me, pointing down the stairs into the basement.

"I didn't even know there was a basement," I told her.

"Mom hated it down there too. We pretended it doesn't exist."

I raised my eyebrows and made a mental note to carry the suitcase all the way down at some point and see what else might be down there. For now, we locked the door and pursued our Saturday evening plans, which included ordering a pizza and watching a movie of Diantha's choosing on television.

That night, Diantha asked me to tuck her in, and I tried my best not to let her see how touched I was to be let into her life this way. It was actually the first time I'd been let into her room.

The walls were adorned with an interesting mix of pop culture paraphernalia. A Taylor Swift poster covered one deep purple wall, and a Stevie Nicks poster hung right next to it. On the other wall was a shelf full of big bobble-headed statues—all of them from Star Wars. There was a table next to her bed with a Lego creation half-built on top of it, and a shelf full of novels next to that. Diantha, it seemed, was interested in a wide variety of things, and the knowledge gave me a warm little glow in my chest.

I sat on the edge of her bed as she pulled her fuzzy blankets up to her chin, and I wondered—not for the first time—about her father. Daisy had never told us who he was, or what had happened to him. A tiny sliver of fear shot through me as I looked down at my niece, her face scrubbed clean of makeup making her look so young and innocent. Would some man one day come to claim her as her father? Take her away?

I suppressed a shiver. That was a mystery to be solved another day and a worry it just didn't pay to harbor. For now, I felt some triumph in having managed the first step in solving the mystery of befriending a tween girl.

"Aunt Dolly?" Diantha asked, looking up at me from her pink pillow.

"Yes?"

"Now that we know each other a little bit, do you think you could please call me Danny like everyone else?"

I laughed. "I think I can manage it, if that's what you'd prefer."

"It is," she said with a smile. "But does that mean I have to call you Aunt Dahlia, because you prefer it?"

I took a moment to reply, letting the answer bubble naturally from within me. I thought it surprised us both when I said, "Actually, I think maybe here in Saltcliff, I am more of a Dolly."

Chapter Ten

The next morning, Danny was up early with me, helping me bake off the muffin dough and scones I'd prepared ahead of time.

We chopped vegetables and I helped her make a crust, and we also prepared two big quiches and a pan full of bacon. I adored the new kitchen I had to work in—the one in my apartment had been tiny, with only a four-burner electric stove. The inn had gas burners—six of them. And having two ovens was a gift from baking heaven.

By eight a.m., we were setting up the side table in the inn's dining room for guests to serve themselves from. At nine, we had a full table of diners and Amal stepped through the front doors looking calm and refreshed.

"Everything looks amazing, Dahlia. You're getting the hang of things quickly," she told me, nodding to the buzz of happy eating guests scattered through the first floor of the inn.

"Thank you," I said. "I had some help. Danny is a great baker and chef."

Danny glowed at my side, and Amal and I exchanged a look. Maybe I wasn't going to be completely useless at inn keeping and being an aunt after all. I desperately hoped not since this would be my occupation for the next decade if all went to plan.

My niece and Taco disappeared back into the apartment once breakfast was concluded, and Amal and I cleared plates and then took a moment to check the books.

"The Robertsons check out today," she said, pointing to the line on the spreadsheet where this was detailed. "And the Smiths and Corpuses. And we should be seeing a new family—the Christies, who have two college-aged children joining them—they will check in Monday. They have three rooms reserved, so we'll be nearly full through Wednesday."

Everything she said made sense, and my confidence was boosted further. We'd strip beds and clean rooms around noon, remaking the rooms for the next guests.

"Do you think we'll be finished by two?" I asked.

Amal shrugged. "Since no one new is checking in today, there is no real rush."

"Good," I said. "Because we have a party to attend if you're up for it."

Amal raised an eyebrow. "A party?"

I nodded. "Yes, at Madame Teratine's. She invited us both."

A slow smile spread across Amal's face. "Well, you're about to meet some very interesting people, I think."

"I am?"

Amal nodded. "Mrs. Teratine has an eclectic group of friends."

I thought of the women I'd seen gossiping at the bakery in town and wondered if they would be there. "What do you mean by 'eclectic?'"

"Probably better for you to just see for yourself," Amal told me. "But let's just say that with Antoinette's reputation around town, not everyone wants to associate with her."

"I see," I said, recalling the way the women spoke about her. They thought she was a floozy, I knew, and it seemed an accepted fact that she was having an adulterous affair with the man who'd died recently. Only, I wondered if people simply made assumptions or if it was true. I decided that was what I'd find out today.

As the hour of the party approached and Amal and I worked side by side, turning over the first room to be vacated, a thought struck me.

"Amal," I asked her. "If we go to Madame Teratine's and leave Danny here... is that okay?"

"In what sense?" Amal straightened the final corner of the bed and stood up, tilting her head at me.

"Is she old enough to be left alone?"

"Ah." Amal nodded and picked up the folded sheet, tossing it so the bulk of it spread across the mattress. I picked up a corner from the side where I stood to help smooth it over the bed. "I think every parent decides for themselves when it is appropriate to leave their children unsupervised."

I was about to tell her this wasn't especially helpful, but she went on.

"Daisy left Danny on occasion during the daytime, but hadn't felt she was quite old enough to leave her on her own at night. When the inn is full, you could also argue that she is not alone entirely."

I nodded, thinking about that. "But I wouldn't want Danny to have to do any inn-related business in my stead," I said. "And even though the guests are guests... "

"They are still strangers," Amal agreed.

"But she ought to be fine for a couple hours this afternoon, right?"

"I would think so, yes."

"Okay." We gathered up the sheets and towels we'd changed, and the cleaning supplies we'd carried into the suite and headed back out. "I'll meet you at the front door at one forty-five?"

"I will see you there," Amal said with a smile. I

followed her downstairs and headed through the apartment door to get changed. Inside, I spoke to Diantha, who brushed off all mentions of my concern at leaving her alone.

"It's the middle of the day," she groaned when I asked if she was scared alone in the house.

"Even with the..." I hesitated to mention the ghost upstairs.

"Mr. Brown?" Diantha laughed. "Harmless."

"You're sure it's okay?"

"Go. Have fun."

I met Amal at the door as agreed, and headed together to the little Spanish style house on Mace Street. As we approached, music and laughter could be heard from a few houses away. A little jolt of nerves exploded inside my stomach. Parties were not my strong suit, and the sounds of people enjoying themselves together and laughing launched all my insecurities to the front of my mind. I gripped the bottle of wine I held more tightly as we let ourselves through the little gate out front and approached the front porch, where two men and a woman—all dressed in bright colors and holding cocktails—were laughing together.

"Well, hello," one of the men said, seeing us approach. He wore a peacock blue sport coat with lime green pants and loafers, and a sizable tricolor Basset Hound lounged at his feet at the end of a sparkly leash.

Taco bumped my leg as if alerting me to the other dog's presence.

"Hello Sylvan, how are you?" Amal said, stepping near and hugging the man.

"Can't complain," he said, grinning as he stepped back. "No one would listen if I did!" His gaze swung to me as the other man stepped forward, a hand extended.

"I don't believe we've had the pleasure," he drawled in a strong southern accent. "I'm Louis, and this lovely creature is Willow. We run Frolic and Frills over on Ginger."

I was about to introduce myself, but Louis began talking again. I swallowed down my nerves.

"Let's see, you're here with Amal, and you're the spitting image of our dearly departed Daisy, so you must be the legendary sister. Daffodil, was it?"

Legendary? Daisy spoke of me? To these people?

"No, silly," Willow swatted his arm. "Delphine. No. Dogwood. No. It's a D flower." The woman tapped a lacquered fingernail to her shiny pink lips as her big eyes looked skyward.

"This is Dahlia," Amal supplied.

"So lovely to meet you, Doll," Sylvan said, pulling me into a hug I clearly had no choice about. "So sorry for your loss. We all loved our Daisycakes." He stepped back and then added, "especially Luigi." He indicated the Basset, who did not seem particularly invested in the conversation as he groaned and rolled to his side.

"Hello," I said, finally able to get a word into this chatty group. "I'm Dahlia, and this is Taco."

"He is very handsome," Louis said.

"Majestic," Willow told me.

I stifled a laugh. Taco was rarely majestic, but I didn't want to take such a glorious compliment from him.

"Thank you," I said.

We were at the point in every conversation where my extreme awkwardness sets in, where there is something one is expected to say to make the leap from initial introduction to sparkling conversation. I never knew what that thing was, and was about to comment on the weather when a wild commotion of bright yellow, orange, and hot pink whirled out the front door.

Madame Teratine. "You're here! How wonderful it is to see you both again, Dahlia, Amal." She glanced at the gathered group on the porch. "Oh you rude boys," she scolded. "You waylaid my guests and didn't even offer them drinks first?"

She all but swept us though the front door to a large living area where more people were gathered, and Spanish guitar music seemed to come from everywhere at once. I lingered, uncertain whether Taco would be welcome inside.

"Oh, bring him in," she said, noticing me hovering. "I love animals. Emile is allergic, so I haven't had a dog in years."

I followed her inside and handed her the bottle of wine I'd been carrying. "Thank you so much for having us."

"Oh, this was unnecessary," she said with a smile. "But it will not go to waste!" She whirled over to a long table at the side of the room. "Mimosa? Gin and Tonic?"

"A mimosa sounds lovely," Amal said, accepting one and turning to me.

"It does," I agreed, enjoying the feel of the cool long flute in my hand.

"I am so glad you've come," she said, sipping her own drink. "I like to get friends together now and then. It becomes so lonely here with Emile working all the time."

"And is everything well?" Amal asked. "At the restaurant? After..."

Madame Terrine's face dropped for a moment, but then her smile returned. "Very unfortunate," she said. "I wish I could say Mr. Baldwicki was a man I will miss, but that is not the case. Still, he did not deserve what happened. And to think it was intentional..." She shook her head.

I nodded, exchanging a glance with Amal.

"Please enjoy yourselves," Mrs. Teratine said, swooping off to the other side of the room to attend to other guests.

I was about to comment on what she'd said about Baldwicki, but three other women approached, greeting Amal with smiles. She introduced me, and I recognized Valerie from the bakery, and met Lulu and Pearl, who evidently ran the Barkcliff Diner for Dogs.

"It's wonderful to meet you," they told me, then all looked sadly at Amal. "How are you both doing? With everything? We so miss Daisy around town."

Amal dropped her head for a brief instant, but then looked up with a sad smile. "We are getting on, as Daisy wished."

"And," Lulu said, stepping in and lowering her voice slightly. "No service? No celebration of life? We waited to hear..."

Amal shook her head. "Daisy was very clear. We should all just move on. No dilly-dallying around her."

The ladies nodded as if they understood, but the idea gave me pause. Daisy had loved being the center of attention in life. I wondered that she would be any different in death. But, I remembered, I didn't really know my sister anymore.

"Well," said Pearl. "We're so glad sweet Danny will be staying in town, and the inn will stay open!"

"Of course," I said, realizing there might have been worry that I'd sweep in and sell the place, taking Danny away. "I think it's best for her, and I'm really enjoying getting to know Saltcliff and all the people here."

Taco flopped into a pile at my feet, and the women smiled down at him.

"It's kind of Antoinette to have us over so soon after all the things at the restaurant," Amal said.

"Well," Pearl replied, leaning in and raising a hand to her mouth as if she was letting us in on a secret. "It's not like she has anything to be upset about, right? Baldwicki being out of the way means Emile can buy the controlling share of his restaurant and be full owner. It's actually a lucky twist for them, even though of course it's a tragedy."

I felt my face pull into a frown. "But wasn't she...I thought Antoinette and Mr. Baldwicki were..." the words were out before I'd had a chance to think about how suggesting my hostess might be an adulteress would be received.

"Oh goodness no," Valerie cried, turning to me and giving my arm a little pat. "You have to be careful who you believe around town. Antoinette has a way about her. It rubs the snooty crew the wrong way when she's over-friendly with their husbands, you know. And she is very over-friendly. Gives people the wrong idea, for sure."

"She's devoted to Emile," Lulu assured me. "But that doesn't mean she wouldn't use her feminine wiles and French *je ne sais quoi* to persuade people to see things her way now and then." She winked one big-lashed eye at me over her champagne flute.

"I actually thought she and my husband might be... you know," Lulu said then. "When they first moved here."

"You did?" Amal asked.

"Yes. When they were getting the restaurant finished up, she spent a lot of time with Seth. He's a general contractor." This last part was delivered to me, helping me get the lay of the land. "There was a lot of work to be done, and Antoinette was the designer between her and Emile for sure, so she was at the Saltcliff a lot. It turned out she was sweet-talking Seth to get him to give her wholesale pricing on some of the finishes she wanted."

"So her persuasive talents are effective," I noted.

Lulu grinned. "They definitely are. Emile also has his talents of course, but they lie one hundred percent in the kitchen."

"But not in *cleaning* the kitchen," Valerie supplied.

They all laughed, and Pearl squeezed my arm. "The man is like an infant. Can't clean up after himself, leaves everything everywhere all the time. He's a brilliant chef, of course, but what grown man can't swallow a pill?"

I shook my head, doing my best to follow the exuberant path of this conversation.

"I'm surprised it doesn't wear on her, cleaning up after him," Amal noted.

Valerie shrugged. "It would bother me, but she babies him. Grinding up his pills for him, cleaning up after him all the time, making sure his every need is handled so he can go on being the brilliant chef Emile."

"You speak of my darling husband?" Madame Teratine said, appearing at Valerie's side.

"They were all telling us how lucky you are to be so in love," Amal said.

"Oui," she agreed. "I am very lucky."

By the time we were departing the Teratine's house, I was a little bit tipsy and felt warm inside in a way I hadn't in a long time.

"I really liked those people," I told Amal as we walked back to the inn. "Everyone was so... open and friendly."

"It's a good crowd," Amal said. "Daisy and Antoinette gathered people like some folks gather jewels or watches. They collected genuine personalities and didn't bother with others."

"That explains why Madame Teratine has the reputation she does, even though she's clearly devoted to her husband," I said.

"She just doesn't care," Amal confirmed. "I should have known she wouldn't have an affair."

"What would that be like?" I wondered aloud. "To not care what anyone thought." It would be freeing, no doubt. But in some ways, it seemed like it also made Madame Teratine's life more difficult here in Saltcliff.

Chapter Eleven

For the next few days, life took on a rhythm of its own. I'd get up early and bake, then have breakfast with Danny and see her off to school before attending to the business of the inn.

By mid-week, I felt as if I'd been living this life forever, though it did feel in many ways as if I'd simply taken over my sister's life. I slept in her room, looked out for her daughter, and even wore her clothes.

The first time Amal had seen me in a pair of Daisy's wide-leg denim pants with her low-profile sneakers and a colorful blouse that draped in a way I thought made me look effortlessly chic (okay, those were Danny's words), she'd lifted a hand to her lips and her eyes had gone teary. But then she'd smiled and told me that the outfit suited me and she was glad to see Daisy's things getting use.

It was strange navigating my sister's world this way,

and I felt honored that she'd trusted me to do it... I just couldn't help feeling like she was the one thing missing from it all.

Thursday morning I answered a call from the Jane Eyre suite asking to have breakfast brought up. Amal and I exchanged a look—the Christie's adult children were evidently accustomed to being waited on hand and foot, and the family's vacation seemed to include the parents going off on day trips while the "children" lounged in their suites and made constant demands.

We prepared a tray with fruit, muffins, bacon, and coffee, and I took it upstairs. I knocked on the door several times before an answer finally came in the form of a young man with his shirt off and pajama pants clinging to his waist for dear life, slipping even as I stood on the threshold.

"Oh, yeah, great," he said, waving me in.

I did my best to avert my eyes—he could't have been more than twenty-two, and I certainly didn't want him to tell his parents I'd been leering at him or anything.

"Just over there on the desk would be perfect, miss," he said.

I followed directions and then turned, shocked to find him standing just behind me.

"Oh!" I gasped, nearly smacking into his chest.

He chuckled and then his hand rose, and he held up a folded twenty-dollar bill, which he proceeded to tuck into the pocket on the front of my shirt.

"Thanks, honey," he said, his voice dropping low.

"Um, okay," I said, suddenly very uncomfortable. "Tipping isn't necessary. I'm the owner," I told him, fishing the money out of my pocket and stepping around him toward the door.

"Consider it a token then."

"A token?"

"Of appreciation for your beauty," he said, his voice keeping to that odd low octave he'd adopted.

"No thank you." I dropped the money on the table near the door and made my way out, feeling as if I'd been holding my breath the whole time I'd been in his room.

"Ew," I said, stepping back behind the registration desk and feeling a bit like I needed a shower.

"You've met Colton Christie," Amal said. "I apologize, I should have warned you."

I looked up at her. "He didn't really do anything..."

"I think he's practicing his flirting or something," she said. "Did he try to tip you?"

I nodded. "It was just kind of... icky." I glanced over at my dog, who was currently curled into a little pile near the apartment door, sleeping contentedly. "I should have taken Taco." At his name, Taco lifted his head, but sensing no immediate need for his services, he let it drop again.

"They come through every few months," Amal said. "I've grown immune."

"You've known them a long time?"

"Since Colton was about twelve. He was working on his masculine charms back then too."

I laughed, imagining a boy of Diantha's age trying to seduce Amal.

"He was a fan of Daisy's," Amal laughed, wiggling her eyebrows.

I was about to say something else, when the front door bells tinkled, and Detective Owen Sanderson stepped into the lobby. His hair caught rays from the sun coming in from behind him, and the casual smile was already in place.

"Morning, ladies." He pulled the door shut behind himself.

"Hello, Detective," Amal said.

I was going to greet him, but couldn't decide if I should call him Owen, as he'd asked, or Detective, as Amal had done. By the time I'd settled on the more formal, he was already approaching the desk and speaking again.

"I was hoping you ladies might have a few minutes to chat this morning," he said, dropping one arm casually on the desk and tilting his head to one side slightly.

I glanced at Amal, who shrugged.

"Sure," I said. "Want some coffee, Detective? A muffin?"

"Please call me Owen. And I sure wouldn't say no to a muffin and coffee. I think I could smell those muffins from outside. Cinnamon?"

"They're cinnamon caramel," I told him, putting one onto a plate and pouring a cup of coffee at the side table. Amal led us to the seating area in front of the fireplace, since all the guests had gone out to pursue their day's activities, leaving the room quiet.

We sat, and I watched as Owen took a bite of the muffin, and let his eyes slide shut for a moment as he chewed.

"It's a good thing I didn't decide to work at an inn," he said after swallowing. "I'd have to do a lot more running or just get used to weighing quite a bit more. This is incredible. Where do you find these?"

Find them? I wasn't sure what he meant. "I make them," I explained.

"You do?" He looked genuinely surprised. "These are really amazing."

"Thank you," I said, feeling the heat climb my cheeks.

"She's a very talented baker," Amal said, making my face heat more. "We're so lucky."

I stared at my hands in my lap, feeling lucky myself.

"Well, I could just sit and eat muffins all day with no problem," Owen said. "But I actually have a little police business to discuss with you ladies."

"Oh," Amal said, her voice cautious. "How can we help?"

"It's about Daisy, actually," he said. "I hope a couple questions won't be too upsetting."

I met his eyes then, startled as always by the depth of the clear green color they held. "No, it's all right," I told him.

Amal was silent.

"Well, I know she was big into agriculture and flowers," he said. "The garden out front is evidence enough of that, for sure."

"It was her favorite thing," Amal confirmed.

"And I've had a couple folks around town mention that Daisy helped them with gardening things—knowing what to plant with what, and even helping procure more esoteric plants they might want."

"She ordered a lot of things online," Amal said. "And knew some of the nursery owners on the peninsula."

"Okay, right," Owen said, nodding as he took the last bite of the muffin. "Do you know if she kept any records? Of what she ordered, or maybe who asked for what?"

I looked at Amal for an answer. So far, I'd been less than helpful with this line of questioning.

Amal smiled. "Daisy wasn't known for her organizational skills," she said, somewhat fondly. Amal rose and retrieved the book she'd shown me from behind the desk. "She kept this," she said, handing it to Owen. "It was kind of a field journal, I guess. She'd list things she planted out front, make notes and put in pictures. I don't know if she kept any formal records. There is a little potting shed off the back patio too, where she kept a few things. I haven't..." she trailed off, looking to the side for a moment.

"That's okay," Owen said. "Maybe you can just show me the shed in a moment." He thumbed through Daisy's book, seemingly looking for something specific.

"She was part of that group, huh?" he asked, pulling a plastic membership card from the pages of the book.

"What group?" Amal asked, leaning in.

"The Coastal Conservationists, the ones blocking the development down south."

Amal's mouth snapped shut, and she said nothing.

"I guess that deal is done, though," Owen said, looking between us.

"It is?" Amal asked, her eyebrows shooting up. "They're going to build?"

"Oh no, sorry," Owen laughed. "Lana Lake came in to chat today after I tracked her down, and reported that without Baldwicki to sell the land, the suit had been dropped and the developer had moved on."

"So she's glad Baldwicki's gone?" I asked.

Owen shrugged. "Seems like," Owen said. He didn't add anything else and continued thumbing through the pages of my sister's book.

"Can I ask what you hope to find in there?" I asked.

Owen's eyes met mine, and his appeared to sparkle as he smiled. "It's a bit of a long shot," he said. He closed the book and set it in his lap. "I've finally got results in from the coroner's office, and she's been able to identify the poison that killed John Baldwicki."

"So it really wasn't the food poisoning?" Amal asked.

"No, this was either accidental or intentional poisoning with another substance. And we're leaning toward intentional."

"Did the poison come from a plant?" I asked, my mind moving through the implications of that.

"Possibly. I'm wondering if Daisy might have ever ordered a castor bean plant. It's an interesting looking plant—one version has deep purple leaves and really striking seed pods. Of course the entire plant is toxic. Especially the seeds."

I frowned. "Why would Daisy want to grow a poisonous plant?"

Amal shrugged. "We talked about that when she told us about the Death Camas, actually. Lots of plants are toxic—daffodils, for one. Since we don't typically eat them, it seems harmless enough to enjoy the looks of them."

"I guess so." I thought of Chef Teratine's explanation of his forage-to-table concept and the mistake the sous chef had made. It sounded now like it could potentially have been much worse.

Owen leafed through the book, and then let it drop shut on his lap. "Mind showing me that shed?" he asked Amal.

She nodded and walked us out the back door onto the

sweeping deck scattered with Adirondack chairs, umbrellas, and heater stands. Beyond the inn's property was the fence along the clifftop and beyond that, the vast Pacific Ocean.

"Gorgeous view," Owen noted.

"It is," I agreed.

There was a little structure hidden in the trees off the end of the deck, and Amal led us to the door, pulling it open. "She didn't keep it locked. It's mostly just soil and gardening tools, some seeds and bulbs, I think."

Owen used his flashlight to look around, picking up a pile of papers stuffed into a garden pot at one end of the bench. "Receipts," he said, shooting me a grin that made my cheeks heat again.

He poked around another minute or two, but then stepped back out and nodded at Amal, who closed the door once again.

"I'll go through some of this stuff and let you know if I need anything else."

"The book...?" Amal sounded worried suddenly.

"I'd like to keep it, but I'll bring it back unharmed, of course."

"Okay," she said. "It's just... it was very important to Daisy."

"Of course." Owen gave Amal a soft smile as he gathered the things he'd collected and headed for the front door.

"Dahlia, I trust you're settling in?" He paused at the door, smiling at me again.

"Yes, I—I'm trying."

"Well, if you ever want tips on the best places to grab a drink, I'm happy to be your tour guide."

"Um, oh. Okay," I said, unsure what the correct response to this was.

Owen smiled again, and then stepped out, the bells tinkling after him. I turned to Amal, who was smiling at me in a strange way.

"What?"

"The detective just asked you out."

I shook my head. "He did not."

"He did."

"Amal, there was no question. He simply said he'd be happy to be my tour guide of local bars."

"That was an offer."

"I really don't drink much."

"I really don't think that's the point, Dahlia."

My cheeks felt hot again, and I didn't want to think about the confusing feelings Owen Sanderson inspired in me. I was much more worried that Daisy might be somehow involved in his investigation. "Do you think Daisy's in any trouble?"

Something dark passed through Amal's eyes, but then she cleared her throat and lifted her chin. "I don't suppose it matters much at this point."

Maybe it didn't. I still hoped the detective wouldn't find anything linking my sister to a crime.

Danny arrived home from school that afternoon, followed by the familiar figure of the detective on her heels. They were laughing about something as they came bustling through the front door of the inn. I'd spent a good portion of the day crocheting on the back porch, and felt oddly guilty about my lack of activity.

Taco hadn't seemed to mind, lazing in the sun happily at my side.

"Detective Sanderson is here," Danny said, a statement I found a bit pointless, since I could see the detective standing right in front of me. He held Daisy's book in his hands.

"Hello Owen," I said, and then turned to catch Danny before she disappeared into the apartment. "How was school?"

"I'm hungry," she called back, slipping through the door with Taco on her heels.

"Kids," Owen laughed.

"Yeah, I guess. I don't think I've really got the hang of that yet."

Owen smiled widely at me, his eyes lighting. "Well, I don't have any either, but from what my brother says, as soon as you think you've got them figured out, they change."

"That's not very reassuring," I said.

"It's the nature of the beast. They morph and grow—it's what we want for them, right?"

"I suppose it is," I agreed. "Did you find what you needed in Daisy's book?"

"No, but I wanted to get it back to you."

I took the book from him and set it back where Amal had kept it. "Thanks." Owen stood in the center of the lobby, gazing around.

"Can I get you coffee? Another muffin?"

He chuckled, and lifted one hand to the back of his neck in a sheepish gesture I found charming. "That's all right, Dahlia. I did hope you might have a second to talk, though."

"Um, okay."

We sat at opposite ends of the long couch, nerves suddenly jigging inside my stomach. Was Amal right? Was Owen going to ask me out?

"I didn't find what I needed in the book, but the receipts in the shed were helpful," Owen began.

Just then, Danny appeared again out the door with Taco right behind her. She picked up a cookie from the side table and then ambled over to collapse into an arm chair next to the couch.

Owen glanced at her, then continued. "It does appear that she made a pretty big order from a local nursery a few months back."

"And there was castor bean in the order?"

Owen nodded. "There was. Just one plant—not the purple variety, the more common one. Looks like this." Owen unfolded a piece of paper from his pocket, showing a plant with long palm-like leaves and dark berries, or beans.

"So that means...?" I asked.

"It's probably in the garden," Danny said, rolling her eyes as if to say, "duh."

"We can certainly go look," I offered.

"Great." Owen stood and we headed out the front door to search the garden. Taco followed, happy for any reason to go outside. I clipped on his leash as he trotted past, still worried about him going exploring in our new home without me.

Together, the four of us wandered the narrow aisles of my sister's incredible garden, each of us checking the photo now and then to see if we had found something similar. After almost an hour, we met at the gate up front, each of us shaking our heads.

"So if she ordered it, but didn't plant it here, where did it go?" I asked.

"I was hoping you might have an idea," Owen said.

"Mom ordered plants for lots of people," Danny said. "But I remember her telling me she had to take some over to the chef's house a few months ago. Before she... got sick."

Owen and I exchanged a look.

"Do you think Mrs. Teratine would mind us looking through her garden?" he asked.

"Antoinette is very friendly," I said, feeling helpful at last. "I'm sure she wouldn't mind."

Danny and Taco accompanied us on the walk over, and Danny skipped up the front steps to ring the doorbell. It struck me again what a contrast my niece was. The dark clothing, the dark makeup—and the ebullient soul of a little girl.

We all waited, but no one answered, and Danny finally turned and put her hands up. "No one's home."

"Well, we're already standing in the garden," Owen noted. "Can't hurt to look around."

We repeated the same search we'd done at the inn, with just as little luck. The sun was beginning to dip toward the tree line to the west as we stepped out the Teratine's gate and walked back to the inn together.

"Aunt Dolly," Danny said, her voice slow and a little dreamy, as if she wasn't sure about what she was going to say next.

"Yes?"

"Do you remember when we stopped over to say hello last week? And Madame Teratine was in the garden?"

"Yes, why?"

"When she first stood up. She had a plant in her hand."

We stopped walking and the scene came back to me—Antoinette standing to greet us, a plant firmly caught in her grasp, its roots a tangled web beneath her gardening glove.

"You're right, she did."

"Do you remember, did it look like this?" Owen asked, holding out the paper again.

"I mean, it was kinda hard to tell," Danny said. "We weren't really looking for this at the time."

"I don't remember, unfortunately," I said. "I guess maybe it looked similar." I took the sheet from Owen's hand and read the little description beneath it. Ricinus Communis, Castor Bean. "It's a bean," I said thoughtfully. I'd been on high alert for that word since childhood, since many beans were actually legumes. "Think it's a legume?" I asked, half-joking.

"Google knows," Danny said, pulling her phone from her pocket. "Yep. It is a legume."

Owen looked back and forth between us. "Not sure why that matters," he muttered.

"It doesn't, I'm sure," I said. Sometimes I was very fixated on things that could kill me, I supposed.

"Only," Danny said, that same slow tone dragging out

the word. She began to hop up and down. "Doesn't Taco sniff out legumes?"

"That's what he's trained for, yes. I'm allergic." I directed this part at Owen, who still look mystified about where this conversation was headed.

"Well, so if we can find where Madame Teratine put the plant after she pulled it, maybe we'll know whatever you need to know!" Danny continued hopping.

"That was at least a week ago," I said doubtfully.

"Green trash only comes every other week," Owen told me. "Could get lucky. Do you think Taco feels like doing a bit of detective work?"

Moments later, we were heading down the little back alley behind the Teratine's block, opening the small cans with green tops and tilting them downwards for my dog to examine. The smells that emanated from the green cans were wide and varied, mostly fecund scents of grass cuttings and plant clippings decaying in the heat of the enclosed cans under the sun. But none of us could sniff out castor bean, except Taco, who merrily went from one offered can to another as we figured we might as well check the houses around the Teratine's too.

When we tilted down the Teratine's can, Taco let out one sharp bark, and Owen and Danny both jerked their heads to stare at me.

"Well?" Owen asked.

"That's his alert, yes."

"So there's legumes in this can?"

"Pretty certainly, yes." I patted Taco's head, though he already looked quite pleased with himself. For all he knew, I'd been preparing to eat whatever was in the can and he'd just saved my life.

Owen cast about the alley, searching for something. Finally, he opened a garbage can and pulled out a plastic bag that appeared unused. "Mind giving me a hand, Danny?"

He handed my niece the bag and she held it open as he dumped the greenery from the Teratine's can into the bag. When it was full, he offered it to Taco, who alerted once again. Owen tied the top into a knot.

"Okay, I'm going to take this down to the lab. Thank you for your help, ladies." He looked at my niece. "Good work. You could be a detective, Danny!"

Danny glowed with the praise, and something warm spread within me at her smile.

"Owen?" I asked softly. "Is my sister going to be in any kind of trouble?"

He dropped a big hand on my shoulder, and the warmth of it spread through me. "Of course not, Dahlia. Ordering plants isn't a crime."

We walked together to the mouth of the alley and parted ways, Danny, Taco, and I heading back to the inn, and the detective heading off toward the police station.

Chapter Twelve

I spent much of the evening after the detective's departure searching online to learn more about the castor bean plant. As the detective had noted, the entire plant was toxic—from the leaves right down to the odd beans that were actually seeds. It came in lots of different colors and varieties, all poisonous, and it was tracked as an invasive species here in Northern California.

And that last bit made me wonder—as a dedicated gardener, would Daisy be willing to plant something she knew was considered invasive, something the state was actively trying to eliminate? It sounded like the fact that it was toxic might not have bothered her as much. Then again, if she ordered it for the Teratines and not for herself, maybe whatever ethics she held didn't extend to the requests of others.

I wondered how you would poison a person with the plant, and while I worried that my search history was becoming a bit incriminating, I continued searching to learn that ricin was a product of the castor bean plant, and that grinding the seeds to remove the coating produced the deadly powder, which would be easy enough to slip into someone's food. Add to that, it was evidently odorless and tasteless, and I wondered if even Taco would notice it if it were ground up.

The real questions still remained then—who wanted to see John Baldwicki dead, and who had access to his food or drink?

My mind kept turning back to the head of the conservation group. I knew people could be quite dedicated to causes they felt were akin to saving the world, and conservation certainly fit that bill. Lana Lake, I recalled, was the leader's name. Could she have killed Baldwicki to put a stop to the development project?

I pointed my browse to the group's site, and found a photo of Lana Lake on the About Us page. She was a stern-looking woman with clear-framed glasses and dark hair swept up into a ponytail that was much more utilitarian than fashionable. The group was headquartered in Los Angeles, which probably meant Lake lived down south. I did a quick search to see if I could find her address, but came up with nothing. Could this woman have arranged to slip ricin into Baldwicki's food somehow?

Keeled Over at the Cliffside

I was up early Friday morning, preparing for the arrival of a few new guests. As the days lengthened and warmed as we moved into summer, Amal assured me we were heading into our busy season. She said it would be unlikely that we'd have many quiet days until after Christmas.

That morning, guests checking in were greeted with my coconut coffee cake and berry scones, and Danny enjoyed a bit of each before heading off to school.

Amal arrived as Danny left, and warmth filled my chest as I watched out the front window to see Amal hug Danny tightly and then tuck a strand of her hair behind her ear as she bent down to speak to her.

I knew from experience that it was hard losing your mother, but I was glad Danny had both me and Amal. Maybe between the two of us, we could offer my niece enough love and reassurance to arrive into adulthood relatively unscathed.

"Good morning!" Amal called as she stepped through the door, looking elegant as ever in slim-fitting black slacks and a red shirt with ties at the shoulders.

"Hello Amal," I said, happy to see her. She becoming a friend, and I enjoyed her company and guidance.

Taco let out a low groan from his spot next to the door, and Amal walked over to give him a quick rub hello.

"Anything happening today?" she asked.

I shook my head. "Nothing really. The Emma and Holden suites should be checking in this afternoon."

She nodded.

"And I have a question for you."

"This sounds like it will require coffee," Amal said, striding to the side table and pouring herself a cup. "Mind if we sit a moment while it's quiet?" She gestured to the couch and I moved to join her.

"I was wondering," I began, thinking of Antoinette and hoping not to offend Amal with my question. "Would Daisy have been okay with the Teratines planting an invasive and poisonous plant in their garden?"

Amal took a sip of coffee and then put her cup on the table before her. "I don't know," she said. "I know she often helped people order and plant things, but she was also a careful gardener. That said, just because she wouldn't plant it here doesn't mean she'd stop someone else from doing so. Why?"

I explained about the plant I'd learned about yesterday.

"She ordered the castor bean plant. It's suspicious, don't you think? Antoinette asked Daisy for it, planted it, and then pulled it out of the garden just after Mr. Baldwicki's death. As if she no longer needed it, or was…"

"Disposing of incriminating evidence."

"Exactly," I said, hating to think of my new friend this way, but unable to look past the evidence.

"She could have simply changed her mind," Amal said. "But the timing, I agree..."

I shrugged. "Owen knows everything we know, so I guess this is up to the police now."

Though Antoinette seemed a likely suspect, and her husband as well, I still wondered about the absent sous chef. Had Owen found him and questioned him?

The curiosity and my worry about Antoinette made it hard to concentrate on inn business, so at lunchtime, I excused myself, hoping Taco and I might be able to find Owen and see if he'd share any news with me. I leashed up my dog and headed out on a stroll to the little police station, which sat on a street at the top of Saltcliff, presiding from its perch over the rest of the little town.

I was just about to mount the steps of the station when Owen stepped out the front door.

"Dahlia!" he said, and the smile that lit his face seemed genuine.

"Hello," I called, stopping on the sidewalk and deciding I would not tell him I had been looking for him.

Owen bounded down the stairs to meet up, and I couldn't help noticing the athletic way he moved, with an ease and assurance I admired. "How are you and Taco today?" he asked, the smile never fading beneath his aviator shades. His broad shoulders and straight teeth made him look like he belonged in a movie more than he did here at a small-town police station.

"Good," I said, feeling the familiar blush creeping over my cheeks. I was thankful for the ocean breeze that blew by just then.

"I was just heading out to find some lunch. I don't suppose you'd join me?"

"Oh, um." I wanted to say yes, but my mind scrambled in search of an answer for the simple question. What would it mean if I accepted? Was this a date? Was I supposed to play hard to get? "It's ah..."

"I'll rephrase," Owen said, the smile never fading. "Have you eaten yet?"

"No, not lunch. I had breakfast a while ago." If I could have slapped my own forehead without making the situation worse, I would have. He didn't care about breakfast. What was wrong with me?

"And are you on your way to an appointment, or do you have a half hour free?"

"Free," I said. Maybe one word answers were best.

"Would you want to spend that free time finding something to eat with me?"

"Yes," I said, wondering if the bald honesty would be too much.

"Great!" Owen reached for Taco's leash. "May I?"

I felt my mouth drop open just a bit as I handed the leash over. Was walking my dog the equivalent of giving me his arm? It felt chivalrous somehow. I liked it.

We ended up getting a table at a little Italian deli that had a patio on the second floor of a building on the east side of town, on one of the streets Taco and I hadn't explored yet. The patio looked up the hill, rather than down to the ocean, but the view of the charming street and the dense foliage of the trees was just as nice. As was the company.

"How are you finding Saltcliff?" Owen asked. "I'm sure you've made lots of friends by now."

"It is a very friendly town," I said, thinking of Antoinette and her friends at the party. "Most people I've met at least."

Owen nodded as he bit into the long hero he'd ordered. He chewed and swallowed, giving me time to formulate the question I'd wanted to ask him.

"Can I ask about the investigation?"

"You can ask," he said with a wink. "There are probably things I'm not at liberty to discuss."

"Of course," I said, lowering my plate quickly for Taco to inspect. He sniffed and then settled, the drool hanging from his jowls. I wiped his face with my napkin and then folded it, replacing it in my lap.

"He's awesome," Owen said, grinning at my dog, who was now curled up next to me, having accepted that yet again he would not be offered any of the food he'd been asked to check for me.

"He is," I agreed.

"So what are you wondering about?"

"Lana Lake. The head of the conservation group that was battling the development of the marshlands."

"Nice lady. Very serious."

That wasn't quite what I wanted to know. "She seemed to have a pretty clear reason to want Baldwicki out of the way, don't you think? And now that he's gone, the project is off."

Owen nodded. "True."

"So you think she might have done it?" I felt a little bubble of excitement. Could solving a mystery be so easy?

"I did think that," Owen said. "Until she came in to see me."

I frowned. "Why?"

"For one thing, she seemed upset about Baldwicki's death. She actually wanted the whole thing to go to court."

"Why would she want that?"

"Publicity."

I looked down for a moment, my brain spinning. That made sense, I supposed. A big part of conservation was wrapped up in public relations—giving people time to understand the reasoning behind your efforts. "Still though, she had a motive."

"But no opportunity. She lives in Los Angeles, and she hadn't made a trip to Saltcliff since December, when the suit began."

I raised an eyebrow. It seemed like a person could lie easily about something like that.

"We're looking into her bank statements and cell records to confirm, but she lives with her ailing mother and her younger sister, who both said they could vouch for her story."

I was no detective, but it still seemed like Lana could be the best suspect. I took a bite of my sandwich and thought a little more before asking my next question.

"The sous chef," I said. "Did you talk with him?"

"Yep, we did," he said. "Not a happy man."

"Because he got fired?"

Owen put down his sandwich and leaned back in his chair, tilting his chin up to the sun for a moment as if he was thinking. "I think Montrose has been dealt a tough hand in life. Raised by a single dad, kind of an outcast in school, I gather. Friends with Baldwicki, like you said. But it sounded like the victim was Mr. Popularity, while Montrose was always the sidekick, kind of in the shadows."

"They were in business together, though, right? After school."

"Lots of ventures, yeah. But from what Montrose said, a lot of them were long shots, and a couple were downright cons that Baldwicki thought up. By the time he was scraping together money to buy the health food business, Montrose said he'd had enough. He figured he was better off with a steady job, even if it was minimum wage."

"That's why he was working in restaurants?"

"Sounds like, yeah."

"And was it just a coincidence that he was employed at a place Baldwicki was part owner of?"

Owen shook his head. "He said Baldwicki felt guilty about how well things had been going for him since he and Adam had been working together. Said Baldwicki gave him gifts—a watch, good seats at the 49ers game, things like that."

"And a job?"

"And a job. Which the Chef was evidently not too pleased about."

"For good reason, I guess. He said Adam was the one who caused the food poisoning."

Owen tilted his head and lowered his shades. "Sounds like you've been doing a lot of investigating yourself."

My spine stiffened. "Oh, no, sorry. I just—"

"I'm kidding," he clarified, laughing. "It's impressive, actually."

"Oh." I stuffed a potato chip in my mouth, unsure what to say now. I didn't want him to think I was edging in on his work. I'd had plenty of men accuse me of that when I'd been a government contractor, and in my experience, men did not appreciate women showing them where they'd failed. "I didn't mean to step on any toes," I said, hoping Owen wasn't angry.

He shook his head. "I mean it, I'm impressed."

I decided to take his words at face value. Owen had no reason to lie.

"So is Montrose a suspect?" I asked.

Owen's smile dimmed slightly, lifting only one side of his mouth now. "Until I can find a reason why he's not, yes."

"The ricin would have been put in Baldwicki's food several days ahead of his actual death," I said, remembering what I'd read. "Was Montrose with him in the days leading up to his death?"

The smile did that half-lift thing again, which I was starting to see might mean I was getting too close to sensitive information. "I'm working on that," he said. "But what I really want to know is about you. What did you do before you moved here to Saltcliff to become an innkeeper and guardian? And part-time detective?"

It was clear Owen was shifting the subject, and I didn't blame him. "I worked for a government contractor," I began. "As a technical analyst."

I'd expected Owen to divert the conversation again, but instead of becoming bored and finding a reason to conclude our time together, he listened with rapt attention to everything I said as I described my life back in Virginia.

"Forgive me for saying it, Dahlia, but it sounds kind of lonely there."

I stared down at my half-eaten tuna. "It was, if I'm honest. Partially because Daisy and I had stopped speaking."

He nodded, and I continued, voicing words I'd kept only to myself for a while.

"When Grandmother died, she left some money to us," I told him. "We were both grief stricken, but I guess we handled it differently. Daisy took Diantha and disappeared, taking half the money. I didn't know where she'd gone or why. We didn't agree about what to do with the money, and I guess she thought I'd try to control it or something, or tell her what to do with it."

"What did you want to do with it?"

"Invest it. Create a trust for Danny with part of it, set up a college fund. Prepare for retirement."

Owen nodded. "Sounds smart."

"But Daisy thought Grandmother would want us to live for now, not plan for tomorrow."

"Would she? Have wanted that?"

I shrugged. "I don't know. Grandmother was the center between us. I was always cautious. Daisy was wilder, more spontaneous. When it was the three of us, we lived somewhere in the middle. But when Grandmother was gone, it was like we both kind of spun off in our own directions."

Owen nodded.

"Daisy disappeared, and I had to make some decisions

for myself. So I took the job in Virginia. I thought getting away would help with the grief."

"Did it?"

Owen's attention was still completely focused on me, his shades discarded for now on the table next to his plate, and those green eyes focused intensely on what I was saying. It was both startling and comforting. I shrugged. "I missed the life we'd had before in Oregon. I missed having a home, I guess. And I missed my sister, but I didn't know where she'd gone."

"When did she come here?"

"About a year after Grandmother died, she sent me an envelope with a picture of Diantha, and the address of the inn. But no message, no note."

"That's odd."

"It was." I dropped my eyes, the familiar confusion and pain of being abandoned ripping through me again. Taco rose and leaned into my legs, always able to sense when I was upset.

"Oh, man." Owen was pushing back his chair abruptly. "I'm so sorry, Dahlia. I hate to run like this, but I lost track of time."

I swallowed the emotion, Owen's quick change of mood making it easy. "That's okay."

"I really enjoyed seeing you," Owen said with a smile. "Let's do it again soon." And with that, he was gone. I turned to look off the patio toward the street below, and saw him jogging back in the direction of the police station, his body moving with practiced ease.

I sat back down and finished my sandwich, my mind doing its best to process the conversation we'd just had.

Taco and I were making our way back to the inn when we encountered a familiar face on the street outside the Saltcliff Apothecary. Two faces, actually, if you counted that of Luigi, the Basset Hound, which Taco surely did.

"Well, hello stranger," Sylvan greeted me from behind heart-shaped sunglasses. Today he wore a bright yellow blazer with pink pants and black and white wingtips.

"Sylvan, how are you?" I asked him.

He pulled me into a quick hug and then dropped an air kiss on either side of my head, an action that made me laugh.

"What? I can't say hello properly to a new friend?"

"You can," I said. "I'm just... I'm getting used to it."

"No proper greetings in stuffy Virginia at your government job, I suppose," he said, what I thought was a teasing tone in his voice.

"No, not really." I thought of Steve back at the office

and tried to imagine him air kissing anyone. The thought made me smile.

"What are you up to this lovely afternoon?" Sylvan asked, tucking his arm through mine and turning us in the direction of the inn to stroll.

"I was just headed home," I told him. "I had lunch with Detective Sanderson."

Sylvan pulled us dramatically to a stop, nearly sending the woman walking behind us crashing into me. "No you did not!" he exclaimed.

I looked around, a little shocked at his apparent surprise. "I did," I said quietly.

"Stop it right now," he said, taking my arm again. "Tell me everything."

I explained how Owen and I had ended up having lunch, and Sylvan oohed and ahhed all the way through what I thought was a very basic story.

"You do know he is the single most eligible man in town, right? All the ladies have been trying to land that green-eyed hottie for years."

I turned to regard Sylvan, but it was clear he was serious. I could see why Owen would be popular. I just wondered why he was single.

"I didn't know that."

"Well, it's true, and you can be sure that the brunch crowd will be wanting all your secrets."

"The brunch crowd?"

"Those horrid plastic women who spend their mid-mornings out in front of Valerie's gossiping."

I realized he meant the women I'd heard saying things about Madame Teratine the day I'd stopped for tea. "Oh, them."

He made a face and a tsking sound. "The scourge of Saltcliff."

I was about to respond when Sylvan pulled us to a stop in front of a pink building with a yellow and white awning. The window had a white decal proclaiming it to be the "Paw Spa."

"We've arrived," he said, both to me and to Luigi, I thought. "It's Luigi's weekly massage and pedicure." Sylvan shrugged as if there was nothing he could do but pay for his dog to have spa services I wouldn't even pay for myself.

"Oh. Well."

"Has Taco been in yet?" Sylvan indicated the fancy dog spa.

"No, he's more of a natural type, I guess."

Sylvan looked down at Taco, considering. Taco, for his part, grinned up at him, letting his tongue fall out one side of his mouth.

"Well," my new friend said, lowering his heart shades. "It was wonderful to see you. I want to hear every juicy detail of your developing entanglement with the detective."

"Um. Okay," I said, startled all over again when Sylvan repeated his greeting as we parted ways, abruptly hugging me and air-kissing.

"Ta!" He called, taking Luigi through the door of the spa.

I headed back to the inn, feeling a bit like I'd just spent a few hours in someone else's life.

Chapter Thirteen

Amal and I attended to the business of the inn for much of the afternoon, greeting guests as they appeared and helping them get settled.

It was nearing sunset when Taco let me know he'd appreciate a stroll, and I realized I still hadn't been down to the waterfront.

It was the perfect day to visit the beach, with the afternoon's warmth beginning to fade as the sun arched over the water. Since Saltcliff sat atop a natural bay, the ocean rushed in to meet the sloping cliff bottoms in a half-moon, giving tourists a perfect swath of protected sand on which to walk dogs, play frisbee, or enjoy the sun.

The warmth had brought out many like-minded residents and visitors, I found, as Taco and I picked our way down the fairly steep sanded slope to the water's edge. The Cypress pines and Eucalyptus trees that made this area popular with artists stretched their iconic limbs against the crystal blue sky and I felt a settled, peaceful glow I hadn't noticed in myself previously. I liked it here.

Taco and I stopped for a moment at the bottom of the slope, and I took off my sneakers and socks and rolled up my jeans. But as soon as the surf washed over my toes once, I decided to stay on the firmer sand above the waterline. It was much colder than the Atlantic. I'd known this, of course. One glance at a map illustrating the directions of the Gulf Stream and the Kuroshio explained why that would be true—but the lore about California beaches had me wondering. I guessed all those surf-crazed singers of the sixties going on about beach blanket bingo didn't mind the frigid temperatures. I gazed out to where several brave souls surfed the breaking waves in wetsuits and wondered if they'd all have hypothermia soon.

Taco trotted happily along, dancing with the line of surf as it flowed in and ebbed back out. He challenged it, dropping low and then springing up when it came towards him again, an endlessly entertaining game of tease and chase.

"Come on, silly," I called, tugging him a little to get him to pick up the pace once more.

"Aw, he's just a puppy, huh?" A friendly voice came from behind me and I turned to see a young woman with a yellow lab on a leash smiling down at Taco's antics.

"He's four, but he seems to be unaware that he's not actually a puppy now."

"Labs are puppies forever," the woman said. Her baseball cap and sunglasses partially obscured her face, but her smile was evident.

"I'm afraid you're right," I agreed. When she made no move to continue her walk, I figured it might be the right thing to introduce myself.

"I'm Dahlia," I said.

"Oh hello." She stuck out a hand to shake. "I'm Abbey Santos, and this is Timber."

"My dog's name is Taco. He's a service dog, though he is doing his best to pretend otherwise right now." Taco had flopped over in the wet sand and was letting the tide wash in around him. He appeared to be out of his doggy mind with ecstasy, and a second later, Timber had joined him.

Abbey and I stood side by side for a little while, as the dogs introduced themselves and leapt around one another.

"Do you live in town, Dahlia?"

"I do." I told Abbey about the inn, waiting for her to tell me she'd known and loved Daisy like everyone else, but she did not.

"I run Tidepool Books on Nutmeg," she said.

"I love bookstores," I told her.

Abbey grinned at me. "Have you gotten to visit any of the nearby towns?" Abbey asked. "Daring Cove or Hammer Valley?"

"Not yet," I said.

"They're both super cute," she went on. "But you're lucky to be in Saltcliff. This is really the heart of this area. Isn't it adorable?"

"It is. I feel like I've stepped into a book, actually."

"Exactly!"

As the dogs settled down, another woman strode toward us across the sand, her floppy hat covering much of her face. I recognized her however, by the thin greyhound by her side. Tessa and Albert.

"Hello there. Abbey, I see you've met Dahlia."

"Yes, we were just getting to know each other and talking about what a sweet place this is to get to live." Abbey said.

"Well, you might change your minds about that," Tessa said sourly. "I take it you haven't heard."

"Heard what?" I asked.

"Chef Teratine is dead. Saltcliff on the Sea is becoming a hotbed for murder!"

My mind had been awhirl since bumping into Tessa on the beach. She hadn't known the details, but evidently the entire neighborhood was buzzing about the Chef having been discovered on his kitchen floor after he didn't show up to prep for the dinner service at the Cliffside.

I imagined Madame Teratine discovering her husband dead, and felt sympathy for the woman. Everyone at the party had exclaimed over how much she loved and doted on her husband... how must she be feeling now?

Taco and I walked back to the inn with a slight detour, past the Teratines' house.

The front gate of the house stood open, and there was yellow crime scene tape along both sides of it. Just as Taco and I stepped close to the opening, Owen Sanderson emerged from the house.

"Dahlia," he called, his usual wide smile in a grim line. "You heard."

I nodded as he strode down the path, his long legs eating up the space between us quickly and bringing him to stand before me. The sunlight caught strands of gold in his sandy hair as the green eyes took in my face.

"Is Madame Teratine doing all right?" I asked him, imagining her inside, crying and wringing her hands.

"Well, that's the thing, actually. She's not here. No one can find her."

Oh. Well, that changed things a bit. "And the chef? Was this... natural?"

"Same symptoms as Baldwicki. We have to wait for the reports, but it looks like poisoning."

"Murder," I said softly.

"I think so," Owen said.

"If Madame Teratine didn't find him, who did?" I asked.

"Neighbor kid saw him on the floor through the window and called 911. He didn't go in, though. He's pretty shaken up."

"I guess," I said, thinking about that and feeling glad it hadn't been Diantha who found him. "I just saw Madame Teratine Sunday," I told Owen.

His eyebrows rose and he turned me down the sidewalk, taking my elbow in his big hand. A little jolt ran through me at the contact, but it wasn't unpleasant. "How did she seem? Distracted?"

"Not really," I said, thinking of Antoinette flitting among her guests in her bright attire, wearing an even brighter smile. "She seemed happy."

He nodded. "Did she say anything to you about a trip? Going away?"

"Not a word. We talked about plants and Daisy, mostly. Looked at the garden a little. It was a party. Amal was with me."

The detective nodded, and we came to stop in the shade of a large tree at the corner of the Teratines' property.

When Owen said nothing more, I asked him, "Do you think these murders are related?"

He made a clicking sound and then said, "I'm guessing

they are. The chef was my lead suspect in Baldwicki's death. Now we're back to square one."

"He was?" I asked, not surprised but still curious to hear Owen's thinking.

"So far, yeah. He had the most to gain, with the ownership of his restaurant coming back to him if Baldwicki died."

"You mean he'd have the chance to buy it back."

"Right. And if Baldwicki was making moves to push him out..."

"I suppose that's a motive," I agreed. "So who are you looking at now?" I asked, not really expecting him to answer. After all, I wasn't part of this investigation in any real way.

"Well, we need to speak to Antoinette. She was involved with both men. I'm just not sure about motive."

"I don't think she was involved with Baldwicki." The words were out before I considered that I really didn't know my new friend well at all.

"We have eyewitnesses putting them together several times prior to his death," Owen said softly, as if he was sad to break this news to me.

I made a mental note to learn more about her time with Mr. Baldwicki. I didn't know her intimately, but I didn't think a woman who talked about her husband the way Antoinette did would take a lover... or kill her husband.

Oh, poor Antoinette. I wondered if she knew her husband was gone. She'd be heartbroken.

"Well if she was involved with Mr. Baldwicki, why would she kill both her lover and her husband?" I spoke my thought aloud.

"Right. I don't know."

"Who else is there?"

"The Teratines have a daughter we're tracking down," Owen said, glancing back at the house, where several men were carrying a covered stretcher out the front door and loading it into a vehicle. "And the restaurant staff needs to be questioned..."

"That makes sense," I agreed. "I guess the real question lies in the links between the two men. If we're looking for one murderer, that is."

Owen smiled at me then, the expression slightly higher on one side than the other—something I hadn't noticed before. There was something about the asymmetry that was charming. "You really do think like a detective, Dahlia."

I felt the flush in my cheeks at his praise. "I'm just good at puzzles," I told him.

He seemed to think about that a moment, his gaze shifting to the horizon, where the Pacific rolled endlessly in and out. Though the trees at the end of the street blocked our view, there was an awareness of it, all that power just down the slope from us. "You know, my second detective departed recently, and we're a small department."

I nodded. It made sense that Saltcliff was a small force. I couldn't imagine there were many crimes here in general, although recent experience seemed to contradict the assumption.

"I wonder, would you be willing to be kind of an unofficial investigator?"

The question surprised me. "What would that entail?"

"Nothing dangerous, I assure you," he said quickly. "Just... it helps to have a sounding board in cases like this. Someone else whose mind works in a particular way to help suss out theories and ask the right questions."

"What would I need to do?"

"Totally up to you, of course, but I'd love a second set of eyes and ears when I talk to the restaurant staff."

I nodded. "I can do that," I said. "Of course, I've got the inn, and Diantha..."

"Nothing that would pull you away from your obligations, of course."

I liked that he thought I would be capable of helping with this, and I couldn't fool myself—I liked the idea of spending more time with the handsome detective.

"Sure," I said. "I could do that."

He nodded and turned us back down the sidewalk toward the house. "Of course Taco's observations will be welcome too," he said.

full of papers. There were three stools shoved against the wall under the light switch, each of them similarly loaded with paperwork. Owen gathered the papers and pulled two stools out for us to sit on.

"Now then," Owen said to the girl who appeared terrified. "Your name is...?"

"Sophie Miller." Her voice shook as she spoke, and I realized the girl was probably closer to Diantha's age than my own. I nudged Taco with my foot and he moved to the girl and dropped his big head on her lap, looking up at her with his mournful eyes. "Oh!" she laughed, and glanced at me, and then dropped her hands to his soft ears. "Hi buddy."

Sophie visibly relaxed with Taco's help, and Owen continued questioning. "Were you working the lunch shift the day diners were sickened by poison?"

She shook her head. "No sir. I go to school most days. I work weekends and dinners."

"Were you working last night?" Owen asked.

"Yessir. I was here from four-thirty to twelve-thirty."

"And did the chef depart before you?"

"Yes. He left around eleven, I think," Sophie said, one hand still rubbing Taco's ear.

"Did you notice anything strange about him last night or in the evening before? Was he distracted, or worried?"

She nodded. "I think he was, yes. And he was sort of... I don't know, wobbly?"

"Wobbly?"

"Yes," she said. "And he had a cough."

Owen nodded, making a note in his phone. "How long had you noticed the cough?"

"Yesterday and the day before for sure. I thought it was probably not great for him to be working around food if he was sick."

"Did he mention feeling sick?"

"Not to me, no."

"So you weren't working on the day everyone was accidentally poisoned, but I assume you'd worked with Adam Montrose in the past? The sous chef?"

She frowned. "Yes. We both started when the Cliffside opened."

"You didn't like him," Owen guessed.

"He was... " Sophie blushed and looked down at Taco's head in her lap. "He was inappropriate sometimes. With me and the other women."

Owen made a little clucking noise.

He continued asking questions, mostly about what Sophie was studying and what she hoped to do when she graduated, and I let my gaze wander the crammed piles of papers and letters sliding from the chef's desk.

One sheet of paper was barely hanging on to the desktop, its corner trapped under a pile of other items. I had to tilt my head a little to read it, but the more I perused, the more interested I became in what was on it.

The sheet appeared to be a resume, but there were several handwritten notes scrawled across the page. One was at the very top where the resume owner's name appeared. The resume read: Sally Trenton, Acclaimed Food Critic. But the red ink accompanying the title slashed through it violently and the word next to it said, "Fraud."

Next to each entry on the page was a similar note, but these appeared to be more like research references.

I craned my neck a bit more, glancing at Owen to ensure he wasn't worried that I wasn't listening as Sophie described how she hoped one day to work with animals somewhere in the country. Next to New York Cuisine Magazine, the red ink read: No record of Sally Trenton ever employed. Near the bottom, in the education section, Culinary Institute of America was accompanied by an arrow with the words "never graduated" penned at its side.

I waited for Owen to excuse Sophie and did my best to give her a kind smile as she departed, but then I snatched the sheet out from under the pile, a couple others falling from beneath it as I did so.

"What's going on over there, Dahlia?" Owen asked, smiling in a way that told me he knew very well I'd been distracted.

"Sorry," I told him, picking up the other sheets that had fallen. They were photocopies of the one I'd been reading. "Something caught my eye."

"Let's see."

I handed Owen the sheet I'd been reading and turned my eyes to the photocopy I'd picked up.

"So this Sally Trenton might not be quite the food critic she claimed to be."

"And," I said, my brain kicking into high gear, "if I'm not misremembering, she's the one who gave the Cliffside a bad review when it first opened."

"You think the chef checked her out after the review panned his new venture?" Owen asked.

I shrugged. "I suppose I would do the same."

"And he found out she wasn't quite what she was presenting herself to be."

I nodded.

Owen looked thoughtful as he read the rest of Sally's redacted resume. "Has she been reviewing restaurants lately?" he asked.

I pulled out my phone and ran a search on her name. "Looks like she does them pretty regularly," I said, showing him the list on my screen. The most recent was dated the previous week.

"So Chef Teratine didn't expose her…"

"I wonder why not?" I asked.

Owen jotted something down on his phone and smiled. "I knew having you around would be helpful," he said.

We continued the restaurant interviews, Owen ushering in the grumpy host, who rolled his eyes at me and sat down.

The host, Zane, carried himself with a pretentious air that made me dislike him even more than I had the day I'd dined here.

"I don't know what you could possibly think I might know," he told Owen as he sat.

"I expect you know quite a lot. Don't sell yourself short," Owen said, winking at him.

The man flinched, and I hid a smile, realizing that Owen was messing with him. He deserved it, I thought.

While Zane shot nasty looks at Taco, who didn't seem to notice at all, Owen questioned him. He'd been present at the lunch where diners were sickened, of course, and for every meal service since.

"Did you notice anything odd about the chef in the last couple days?" Owen asked.

"The man was always odd," Zane said, sighing.

"In what way?"

"Hiring that wannabe sous chef, for one thing," he said. "The man had never worked in fine dining. He'd been a burger flipper before this, for heaven's sake."

"Why did he hire him?" I asked.

"Who knows? Why did he insist on cooking with weeds from local gardens?"

"He said it was a field-to-table concept," I told him.

Zane waved a hand at me. "I know. He wouldn't shut up about it."

"So if you were unhappy working with Chef Teratine, why did you stay?" Owen asked.

Zane's eyebrows rose and he looked from Owen to me. "Did I say I was unhappy?"

"Maybe it's just your general demeanor," Owen said.

"Is questioning my personality getting you closer to solving your double murder case, Detective?" Zane asked.

Owen chuckled. "Don't leave town, okay?" He gestured toward the door and Zane was gone a moment later. "Pleasant fellow," he said.

"I didn't find him at all pleasant," I said.

Owen's eyes met mine then and he laughed lightly. "Me either. I was being sarcastic."

Right. I should have figured that out. "Sorry. Sarcasm isn't something I'm good at."

Owen's smile didn't falter. "Not a problem. My mother always said that sarcasm was the laziest form of humor."

That gave me something to think about as Owen went out to get one of the line cooks.

By the end of the interviews, we'd learned very little that I thought would be of use, except that the chef had clearly been suffering some kind of ailment in recent days.

"There might be loads of other interesting things in here," Owen said as we prepared to leave. "But it's gonna take a while to go through it all." He gestured at the piles of paperwork. "I've got a guy coming in to sort it all later."

"Looking for something specific?"

"We always try to get a feeling for any sort of financial difficulties or sudden income—those are often suspicious. Personal correspondence or journals can also contain tidbits of information that could lead us somewhere. Nice work on the food critic. We can chat with her next. I suspect the chef may have been blackmailing her somehow."

I felt my eyebrows climb. First murder, and now blackmail? My life had gotten exponentially more interesting since moving to Saltcliff, and that wasn't even counting my new occupation or family obligations.

I glanced around. I didn't see a journal or any personal correspondence, but who knew what was at the bottom of these piles?

"Owen, I know we were thinking that the chef stood to gain if Baldwicki died, but do we know if Baldwicki had a will? Family who might inherit? It sounds like he had amassed a good deal of money."

The detective nodded. "His lawyer has been contacted."

"And what about the chef?"

"We're assuming that'd be his wife. Or his daughter. Looking into it."

"And Lana Lake?"

"Her alibi checked out. And I'm not sure she even knew the chef."

So nothing to do there for the time being.

We headed back out, and Owen locked the front door of the restaurant with what I assumed was the chef's key.

"Thank you for your help today," he said as we faced one another on the sidewalk. It was late afternoon, and the sun was angling over the trees in a way that painted everything yellow and gold.

"What's next?" I asked.

"Next, I need to track down the food critic."

I glanced at my watch. It was already after six, and I'd definitely forgotten about my inn-keeping and guardianship duties while playing detective. "I should get back." I turned to go, but Owen caught my hand, stopping me in my tracks.

My eyes found the spot where his hand held mine, and warmth bloomed inside me. His fingers were strong, elegant but clearly masculine, and seeing them wrapped around mine was oddly thrilling.

"Thanks for this, Dahlia. You were a big help today." He smiled as I looked up, and then released my hand and set off in the direction of the police station.

I stood for another beat, working to calm the strange way my heart had just taken off as if in a race.

Chapter Fourteen

"Is it true?" Diantha was waiting when Taco and I came through the door, energy vibrating from her thin body as I hurried to the registration desk. I had not meant to be away so long, and felt as if I'd been shirking my duties as innkeeper, though no one seemed particularly miffed or eager to speak to me.

"Is what true?" I asked my niece as Taco gulped water in the corner and then flopped down on his bed, clearly exhausted from our stint as private investigators.

"That Chef Teratine..."

I nodded. "Yes, unfortunately."

"How is Madame Teratine?" Diantha's voice was full of sadness, as if it was she who'd lost her partner.

I shook my head. "I don't really know. She's gone. The police are looking for her now."

Diantha tilted her head to the side. "Gone?" She

looked around the lobby, where a few guests lounged on overstuffed chairs or warmed their hands by the always glowing fire, as if she might spot her here. "That's a bit suspicious."

I nodded, though it was possible that Madame Teratine just had poor timing and would be home soon, no doubt bereft at the loss of her husband.

"How was school?" I asked her, feeling more settled now that I'd ensured no one had missed me.

She lifted a shoulder. "Math test. Did okay."

"Good," I said, but then rethought my casual response. I was a parent figure now. "Next time better than okay. We'll study."

"Are you good at math?" she asked me.

That didn't even need a response. I gazed at her, smiling.

"Oh yeah, Mom told me that. She was the reader, and you were the numbers girl."

"Your mom said that?" There was something odd about hearing things Daisy might have said about me, like I was scraping echoes of the past to tuck into a little box for safe keeping.

"Yeah. What's for dinner?" she asked. "Can we go out?"

I felt like I'd been out all day, but wanted to make my niece happy, and she seemed to be settling a bit into the routine of having me here.

"Sure," I said. "Where would you like to go?"

"There's a ramen place in Daring Cove," she said.

"Sounds perfect," I told her.

We secured the inn so anyone entering would need their room cards to open the front door, something Amal had shown me how to do at night or if we needed to leave the place unattended for a long period of time. And then Taco, Diantha, and I loaded into my sister's car, which was parked in the single car garage behind the inn.

I sat for a long moment, the motor running in the little electric blue Fiat and Taco's hot breath on the side of my neck as he leaned over my seat from where he sat in the back. I hadn't driven in quite a long time, but assumed it would come back naturally. Like riding a bicycle. Only, this car was a stick shift.

"Aunt Dolly, do you know how to drive?"

"I do," I assured my niece. "Just reviewing what I know about stick shifts."

"You do know how to drive a stick, right?"

"Yes," I told her. "In theory."

"That's not very encouraging," she said quietly.

"We'll be fine," I told her, and took a deep breath before depressing the clutch and shifting the car into reverse. I felt the gears engage and the motor changed in pitch, and then I applied a tiny bit of gas, and the car rolled smoothly backward. "See?" I asked her, proud of myself.

"We've made it to the driveway. Yay." She pushed the button to close the garage door.

I glanced at my niece. Yes, as I suspected. Sarcasm.

There was a good amount of foot traffic in Saltcliff, and my concern was backing over some poor tourist on our way to the street, but I managed to back all the way out and onto the road without incident. Then, I clutched again and hit the brake, shifting into first gear and pressing slowly on the gas as I let off the clutch. The car lurched and then moved along more smoothly. As the motor turned furiously, I depressed the clutch again and repeated the motion, shifting into second with a bit more finesse.

"I think I'm getting it," I told Diantha. "Now, where are we going?"

Diantha pointed left up Nutmeg. "Freeway."

"Is there an alternate route?" I asked, sweat breaking out on my forehead at the suggestion that I should take us on the freeway. "Side streets?"

"Nope."

After a half hour of white knuckle driving, during which I stalled the car only four times—mostly at stop signs on the approach to the freeway and once getting off, we had arrived in Daring Cove. As soon as there was an opportunity, I pulled over and let the car idle, taking a few deep breaths.

"You did fine," Diantha said, patting my arm.

Her praise erased a bit of the tension, and after

stretching out my fingers and neck, I was ready to begin again.

We navigated toward the waterfront. Daring Cove was not guarded by the same protective cliffs that surrounded Saltcliff, and the town had a main street that ran parallel to the waterfront, which boasted a wooden boardwalk jutting into the sea, and a smooth, wide swath of beach. There were several streets set back a bit, and each one featured many little cottages, each painted in candy colors and nestled in close together.

My niece and I sat across from one another in the tiny ramen shop, each of us in front of a large bowl of soup filled with broth and noodles and vegetables. It was quiet inside the little hidden shop, but there was a peaceful air about the place. Taco nestled at my feet, and I was about to ask Diantha more about her day when I heard her sniff.

"Danny?"

She looked up at me with big sad eyes, the dark makeup only serving to make her look even more tragic.

"Are you all right?"

She shook her head, and then her thin shoulders crumpled as she cried. A tiny choked noise escaped her, bringing Taco to his feet immediately. He moved and put his head on her lap.

"Taco," she half-sniffled, half-laughed.

"You thinking about your mom?" I guessed.

I could only see the top of her head, but it nodded.

"Yeah. We came here a lot." She sniffed loudly and then looked up at me, and something in my chest cracked at the pain in her expression. "I thought coming here would be like you said—a tribute to Mom. Eating things she liked, remembering her. But I just miss her."

I nodded, not sure what to say. I didn't ever want Diantha to feel that I was trying to supplant Daisy in her memory or in her life. But I didn't know much about my sister's last years, and there wasn't a lot for me to add that might be helpful.

"You promised it would get easier." This was a hope-filled plea, not an accusation.

"I know that it will. But it takes time."

She sniffed again, her hands buried in Taco's fur as he all but climbed into the chair to comfort her.

"I think grief is one of those things that sort of moves in to stay," I said, thinking of my own experience of losing Grandmother, and of losing Daisy a decade earlier—even though she'd still been alive then. "It's something you learn to live with, to make room for. The longer it stays, the more you get used to it, and the less room it takes up. But then there are days now and then when it wants to remind you it's still there. And those are the hard days."

We were quiet a minute, and then I added, "It's like having a roommate who's quiet most of the time, but who occasionally leaves dishes in the sink and plays loud music." I shrugged. That was the best I could do, I thought.

Diantha looked up at me and one side of her lips curved up, despite the tears in her eyes. "Like having a bad roommate?"

"I'd do better writing an equation for it," I said.

She let out a little laugh. "I think the roommate thing is pretty good, actually."

"I promise it'll get better, Danny."

"Your analogies, or the grief?"

"Hopefully both."

The smile dropped again, and she looked down, taking a deep breath. When she met my eyes again, hers were full of worry. "I feel like if it gets easier, that means I'm forgetting her. I don't want to forget Mom."

I shook my head. "You'll never forget her. You'll just find different places to keep the memories so they hurt less. They'll change. But you won't ever lose them."

Diantha sniffed and nodded, and a few minutes later, she'd picked her chopsticks up again and resumed eating, but her sadness lingered within me, as if I'd helped her by absorbing some of it myself. Was this what parenting entailed?

The following day, I rose early to bake the banana bread and cinnamon rolls I'd made Thursday, and to prepare the eggs and sausage links I planned to put out.

Amal was already getting the coffee brewing when I stepped through the little door out into the lobby, and we exchanged a smile.

"How was your night?" I asked Amal, who looked every bit as elegant and put together on a Saturday as she ever did.

She turned to me with sad eyes and a smile that probably wasn't a real smile. "It was fine," she said.

"You are thinking of Daisy."

She nodded. "We spent a lot of time together," she said. "My days feel a little empty now. It'll get better."

That made sense. I was about to find something to offer her verbally, some platitude I thought people might use in this situation, but she saved me by speaking first.

"What are your plans today?" she asked.

"I need to check in at the bank if it's open," I said. Daisy had left Post-It notes on the checkbook to let me know that my name had been added to the accounts for the inn and for Diantha's college savings, but that I'd need to physically present myself to finish the paperwork.

Finding the notes had actually set off something inside me I wasn't quite ready to address. My sister had prepared for my arrival, it seemed. She'd left me notes about banking. Logistics. But nothing else. Nothing... personal.

I had worked hard the evening before to overcome any offense at the thought that Daisy might have taken the time to write a letter. But then again, perhaps it had been all she could do to write the notes. She'd been sick, after all.

I pushed down the thoughts and asked Amal, "Are they open Saturday?"

"I think so," Amal said. "The branch here in Saltcliff is probably open reduced hours on Saturday."

"Okay," I said, thinking aloud. "So I'll take care of that this morning. And then I'd like to chat with the detective, maybe."

"Any leads on your big case?" Amal smiled as she asked this.

"Actually, Owen included me yesterday in a semi-official capacity."

"He did?" Amal's easy smile dropped along with her jaw.

"Yes. He asked me to be a second set of eyes and ears on the investigation since they're so short-staffed at the department."

"Wow," Amal said. She was sorting through the tea bags lined up in the flat box atop the side table, her long fingers ticking through them one by one. "He's an attractive man," she said, and I wondered about her intentions in saying so.

A strange spike of warning flared inside me—some primal instinct I wasn't sure I'd felt before. Was it...jealousy? I forced myself to sound reasonable, hating the sudden emergence of the ugly emotion. "Well, I hear he is single and considered very eligible. You should get to know him."

A warm laugh escaped her as she looked up at me over her shoulder. "Not for me, Dahlia. For you."

She might as well have pinched me. The inescapable flush flooded my cheeks and even the skin on my arms felt suddenly warm and tight. "I, uh. I suppose. I mean..."

"Just an observation," she said soothingly. "I didn't mean to make you uncomfortable."

I shook my head, cleared my throat. "I'm fine, I just..."

"You'd thought about it. How attractive he is."

"Not in any concrete way," I assured her.

"Dahlia." Amal stepped near. "There's no commitment or assumption in mentioning aloud that someone is pleasant to look at."

"Right."

"And he is, isn't he? He's tall and strong, and you can't argue with those green eyes, right?"

A smile pulled at my cheeks and I felt just as awkward and awful as I had in sixth grade when I'd realized I had a crush on Peter Christensen. That hadn't gone well at all. It turned out adolescent boys didn't appreciate frank honesty as much as I'd hoped. And they didn't necessarily keep embarrassing admissions of interest from adolescent girls to themselves, either.

"I promise not to pry," she went on. "But I wanted to be sure you know you can talk to me if you ever want to."

I nodded, unable to meet her eyes as embarrassment threatened to take me back to childhood, to make me that same awkward girl I felt like I'd been for the last forty years. Why was I like this? I swallowed hard and forced myself to keep my chin up, thinking of the way Owen had taken my hand yesterday.

Amal moved back to finish preparing the coffee and tea just as the first guests came down the stairs for the morning.

She greeted them easily, and I smiled and waved from the registration desk, studying her easy way with near-strangers. A smile. A kind word. A question about their sleep. I could do that, I thought.

Soon, the front rooms of the inn were full of guests chatting, drinking coffee and tea, and eating. Taco remained curled on the bed we'd set for him to one side of the apartment door, and Amal and I attended to checking the departures and arrivals we'd be expecting starting tomorrow. By nine-thirty, many guests had set off for their adventures for the day, and Diantha stumbled out, bleary-eyed.

"Morning," she said, and Amal crossed the space and pulled her into a quick hug.

"Morning pretty girl," she said.

Diantha hadn't put on any makeup yet, and her hair

was pulled away from her face with a thick pink headband. She looked young. And she was pretty. Objectively speaking. I had long been a believer that people should not assume the first thing a girl should be told about herself is how she looks, but I understood where the impulse came from. It was hard to comment on someone's intellect at eight a.m. on a Saturday morning. "Good morning," I said.

"Hi Aunt Dolly." Diantha dropped down next to the door and gave Taco a good rub through his thick scruff. "Hello Taco Dog. Hello, sir. How are you today?"

Taco gazed at her with adoring amber eyes, reveling in the attention she lavished on him. Taco, for one, was living his best life here in Saltcliff. I wondered if he'd been at all lonely with only me for company back in Virginia.

"I need to go to the bank this morning," I told her. "Would you like to come?"

"Oooh, the bank," Diantha said.

"Sarcasm," I guessed.

"Yes," Amal said. "She's really honed her talents."

"Is that a yes or a no?" I asked.

"Can I stay here with Amal?" Diantha asked.

"Of course," Amal and I both answered at once.

I exchanged a smile with the woman who was becoming a friend and a sort of co-parent, thankful she was here to help me navigate my odd new world.

Soon, Taco and I were making our way through the ever-blooming streets of Saltcliff to the Salt Coast Bank, a regional branch of a bigger bank, where Daisy had set up the accounts for the inn and for herself.

I was just finishing up with the inn's business as a man approached the teller to my right.

"I was told I needed to come in and sign to finish setting up the account I opened online earlier this week," he said.

I thanked the young man helping me and turned away, about to leave the bank when the man next to me went on: "My name is Adam Montrose."

The sous chef.

I wanted to linger a moment longer, but had no real reason to do so. Looking around for an excuse, I did the only thing I could think of—upended my bag at my own feet.

Taco stared up at me, and his expression seemed to indicate that he believed I might be losing my mind, and then he ducked his head down, clearly intending to eat a tampon that had fallen to the floor.

"Oh no," I said dramatically, realizing my acting skills could use some work. "Silly me. Just a moment." I dropped to my knees, close enough to hear the teller speaking with Adam.

My own teller leaned over the counter to peer down at the assorted contents of my bag on the floor, and let out a sigh. "Take your time," he said.

I lingered, collecting my belongings with painful slowness as I focused on Adam Montrose and his transaction.

"Yes," the teller explained to him. "For this amount of funds coming in all at once, we require an identification verification and signature."

"I understand," Montrose said. "Trust me, I've never had to deal with this much money before in my life!" He laughed uncomfortably before falling silent again.

I finished collecting the lip gloss and tissue packet, my pens and calculator and reading glasses from the floor, stuffing them all back into my shoulder bag, and stood. "Sorry about that," I told the teller who'd been helping me.

"No worries," he said. "Have a good day, Ms. Vale."

I left the bank, pulling out my phone to call Owen.

He picked up after a few rings, sounding sleepy.

"Did I wake you?" I asked. I guess I should have considered that it was Saturday morning. Detectives probably didn't work weekends. But when they were investigating murder?

"Ah, yeah, a little," Owen said, and I had an image flash across my mind—Owen, shirtless, rising from messy sheets in the rays of the golden morning sunlight. A furious blush flashed up my chest and face. "It's fine. I didn't mean to sleep so late," he laughed. "Long week. What's up?"

"I'm so sorry to bother you," I said, flustered now. "Should I call back Monday?"

"Dahlia, I'm happy to hear from you. It's fine. Tell me why you called." His voice was grumbly and low, and for some reason my tummy flipped on hearing it.

I walked away from the bank, double checking that Adam Montrose wasn't nearby, and then told Owen what I'd just heard.

"Montrose comes into a lot of money immediately after Baldwicki and the chef die," he said, clearly thinking aloud. "That's very interesting."

"It is," I agreed.

"Let me dig into that a bit," he said. "I have yet to hear back from Baldwicki's lawyer, but I'm going to try him again now. Thanks for the call. Have a great day, Dahlia."

"You too," I said, feeling slightly deflated that my part was finished for now as I pushed my phone back into my bag and turned back toward the inn.

Chapter Fifteen

Saturday evening was quiet. Many of the guests were out with dinner plans or other evening activities, and Diantha, Amal, and I ate together in the apartment, and then—at my niece's suggestion—played Scrabble. Evidently Daisy was very good at the game, and it wasn't as if I hadn't played before. But in an effort to make the best possible points combinations with my letters, it was as if I had forgotten the most common of words.

Amal beat us both soundly, in her quiet, elegant, understated way. I admired her. She reminded me of a body of water—calm and smooth in outward appearance, but with worlds of depth beneath the surface. In some ways, she was a bit mysterious, and I wondered about her life outside the inn, which she rarely spoke about. She was old enough to be married, to have a family, but it didn't seem like she had anyone at home. I realized as we played that I didn't even know where she lived.

"Amal," I said, putting out yet another three-letter word.

"Yes?"

"Where do you live?"

She smiled across the board at me. "Nearby."

"Amal lives on Clove," Diantha supplied. "In the cutest little pink cottage you've ever seen."

Clove was only a couple streets away from the inn. "I've probably walked Taco past your house then." I tried to remember a pink cottage, and a few came to mind.

"I'm sure you have," Amal said softly. "I spend quite a lot of time here. Sometimes it feels more like I live at the inn."

Something in her tone caused me to look a bit deeper into her wide dark eyes. "Do you need more time off?" I asked, unsure what she meant.

A little chuckle came from her, but it wasn't a sound I'd classify as happy. In fact, something in the tone, inspired Taco to rise and move to her side, pressing his furry ruff against the side of her legs as she sat on the couch.

"Not at all," she said. "I'm happy to be here. It makes me feel close to Daisy."

I nodded. That made sense. Sort of.

"Quote!" Diantha practically yelled, placing her letters

on the board. "On a double word score. Suck it, Aunt Dolly!"

I stared at her, a little bit shocked by her exuberance. Had she really just told me to suck it?

"Sorry," she said, meeting my eyes and then ducking her head a little. "I got overexcited. That's like a million points, though."

Amal stifled a laugh I could tell was genuine, and I found myself laughing too.

"I'm pretty sure I'm already sucking it without your telling me to do so," I said through my laughter. "You're beating me by more than fifty points. Amal too."

"Mom was right," Diantha said, smiling this time as she mentioned my sister. "You suck at words."

"Thanks a lot," I said. "Maybe you and my sister can go suck it." I didn't think I'd ever told anyone in my life to 'suck it,' but I was getting into the spirit of the teasing.

Amal burst out laughing for real now. "She'd love that," she said. "To hear you say that."

I looked between these two people who'd come into my life so suddenly and laughed along with them, happiness spreading inside me.

Sunday morning I was up with the sun, baking my buttermilk chocolate chip pull apart coffee cake and a tin of "healthy" zucchini bran muffins to go with the egg cups and Canadian bacon I'd set out with fruit.

I was just arranging things on the buffet table in the inn's dining area when the front door tinkled, and I frowned as I spun around. It seemed odd for anyone to be arriving so early and we weren't expecting any new guests until later today.

Antoinette Teratine stood just inside the door, a young woman at her side who might have been her younger sister.

"Antoinette," I said.

"Oh, Dahlia." She crossed the lobby and thrust herself dramatically into my arms, her head dropping to my shoulder as she cried.

I stood still, my arms around this woman I barely knew, trying not to stiffen at the sudden and unexpected contact. The younger woman stood still in the doorway, watching Antoinette sob into my yellow cardigan's shoulder.

"Antoinette, are you all right?" I asked, unable to think of a less ridiculous question. Of course she wasn't. Her husband was dead.

Taco had risen from his bed near the door and approached cautiously. People in need of comfort were historically his domain, and I was sure he was confused about why I seemed to be honing in on his job.

"Mais non," Antoinette answered from my shoulder.

"But you must forgive me. I'm so sorry." She lifted herself from my embrace and stepped back, a hand to her face. "I just cannot..." she shook her head, pressing the manicured hand to her mouth as he eyes squeezed shut.

"Maman," the other woman said, finally moving forward and wrapping an arm around Antoinette's shoulders. "Shhh. It's all right."

I stood awkwardly before this scene as the younger woman comforted Antoinette, and then finally seemed to notice me standing there. "Sorry to barge in. My mother couldn't think of anywhere else to go. I guess we need a room?"

"A room?" I repeated, confused.

"Dahlia, I'm so sorry. I don't know what to do." Antoinette seemed to regain herself, stepping away from what I thought must be her daughter. "Emile is gone, surely you've heard."

I nodded. "I'm so sorry."

"This is my daughter Nadine. I was visiting with her at school when they called me." Her face stiffened. "They suggested I needed to return immediately and that I should not be planning to leave town again." She shook her head furiously. "I am evidently a suspect."

This last was delivered in an indignant whisper-shout as Antoinette's eyes dropped shut again.

"They won't let us stay at the house," Nadine

explained. "It's a crime scene now. Do you have any rooms available?"

Aha. Finally I understood. "I think we will this afternoon," I told them. "Please, have a seat and something to eat, and I'll check."

Nadine smiled at me gratefully as Antoinette whispered, "Merci."

I moved to the desk to pull up our reservations, happy to see that the Atticus suite would be available tonight. It had two double beds—one of only two rooms set up this way.

"Antoinette, Nadine," I said, approaching the women who now sat on the low couch before the fire, which I hadn't actually started yet this morning. "I do have a suite with two double beds opening this afternoon. And you're welcome to make yourselves at home here in the common area until then."

Antoinette looked up at me. "You are an angel," she said. "Please, sit with us a moment."

I dropped into the armchair to one side of the couch.

"I still cannot believe it," Antoinette said quietly, shaking her head. "I said goodbye to him two days ago, and now? I will never see my love again."

Nadine rubbed her mother's back softly.

"It is a shock," I agreed.

"Do you think I might lie down somewhere?" Antoinette asked, gazing around the lobby.

I searched my mind, seeing the irony that in an inn, I didn't have a free bed anywhere. Except, of course I did. "You're welcome to use my room until yours is open," I told her. We were friends, after all, weren't we?

"That is kind," she said. "You are sure?"

"Of course."

"You will be all right?" Antoinette asked her daughter, who nodded and smiled sadly.

I showed Antoinette to my room inside the apartment, stopping to rap lightly on Diantha's door. At the grumble from within I popped it open a crack and let her know that Antoinette would be in my room. She grunted affirmatively, and I headed back out to the lobby.

When I returned, Amal was moving about behind the registration desk. She greeted me with a smile.

"Good morning," I said. "Do you know Nadine Teratine?"

Nadine stood and moved closer. "Hello again," she said to Amal.

"Lovely to see you. I'm so sorry for your loss," Amal said.

Nadine nodded. "It's so difficult to see Maman so upset. And to think of not seeing Papa again..." She looked up at us, her eyes taking on a fierce expression. "And they suggest my mother could have killed him! Isn't that ludicrous?"

It was, I thought. Though we still had no real motive or

suspect for the chef's death. But maybe Owen knew something I did not. "I'm sure they're just being very thorough," I said, trying to console the girl.

Nadine laughed, the tone sharp. "If you'd ever seen my parents together, you'd know how completely ridiculous an idea it is. They were so in love it made you want to throw up half the time."

Her assessment agreed with what I'd learned at the party I'd attended at the Teratines' house.

"And she wasn't even home when he died, so how could she have done it?"

"Ricin is a slow-acting poison," I began, but Amal dropped a hand on my arm and shook her head softly. Maybe she was right. Nadine didn't need a technical explanation of the diabolical workings of the poison that had taken her father's life.

"I'm going to do a little work," Nadine said, and she returned to the couch and pulled a laptop from the backpack she'd brought in with her.

While she did that, I pulled out my cell phone. "I'm just going to take Taco out for a quick moment," I said to Amal, signaling for Taco to join me at the door.

We stepped out into the gray morning and Taco nosed around the garden while I dialed.

"Hello?" Owen's groggy voice came through the line.

"Oh. It's early again, isn't it?"

His sleepy chuckle reached my ear, sending warmth through my chest. "It is. And it's Sunday."

"It is. I'm so sorry."

"Don't be sorry. Sundays are traditionally nice days," he said, and I could hear the smile in his voice. "Sleep in, grab a coffee, wander the village. Maybe have some brunch."

"That sounds nice," I agreed.

"But not when there's a double murder investigation going on," he said. "So what's up?"

I wandered between some tall greenery, the scent of the flowers blooming at my feet wafting around me. "Antoinette Teratine just showed up at the inn. She says she's a suspect?"

"She is," he agreed.

"I guess that makes sense... In both murders?"

"We're still processing the crime scene at the Teratines', and we didn't really have a scene for Baldwicki. Ricin is tough, since it's in the system for days ahead of it actually doing its dirty work. These poisonings could have happened anywhere, but the plant in the Teratines' trash is the best smoking gun we've got right now."

"But Owen," I said, my brain spinning. "Did she have a motive?"

He sighed. "Welcome to the exciting and frustrating world of detective work. Still working on that. Maybe while she's there, you can get her talking a bit."

"Maybe," I agreed, but based on what Nadine had said about her parents' relationship, I just didn't see a motive for Antoinette to kill Emile.

"I'll let you know what comes up," Owen said. "Talking to Baldwicki's lawyer first thing tomorrow. Ask Mrs. Teratine about the food critic. I'll check in with you later to see what you've found out, okay?"

"Okay," I said. "Enjoy your Sunday."

"You too, Dahlia."

I hung up and gazed out over the lush variety of my sister's garden, wishing the answers were somehow more clear.

Chapter Sixteen

The day progressed quickly, filled with guests eating and then checking out to be on with their lives in other places. Amal and I—and even Diantha—turned over the vacated rooms, and we took special care making the Teratines' room as comforting as possible. I set a basket of icebox cookies on the table, added a few extra teabags to the service on the sidebar, and made sure everything was perfect. It was as much a comfort to me as I hoped it might be to my friend. Truth be told, I didn't know what else to do for her.

That evening, I invited Antoinette and Nadine to eat with us in the apartment. Amal had brought a box of chicken pies from a nearby shop (charmingly called "The Chicken Pie Shop"), and we had more than enough to share. Antoinette protested that she wasn't hungry, but then relented when Nadine insisted that a bit of food and company would be good for her.

"Thank you for this," Nadine said as we sat around the dining table in the apartment. "It's very kind of you."

I shook my head. "I wish there was something more… substantial I could do to help."

Antoinette sighed dramatically, her eyes filling with tears as she held her fork over her plate. I steeled myself for another random sob—they'd been escaping her throughout the meal—but she seemed to swallow this one back and go on.

"Who would have wanted to hurt Papa?" Nadine asked, shaking her head.

"Oui, there is no one." Antoinette sniffed and put her fork down.

"A former staff member?" I suggested, thinking of Adam Montrose.

That earned me a sideways glance from Antoinette. "Emile was very generous with his staff. Even those he let go," she said.

I thought of the statement I'd overheard from Montrose at the bank. Surely his severance hadn't been generous enough to warrant the opening of a new account.

"How generous?" I heard myself asking, earning me a stern look from Amal.

Antoinette didn't seem bothered by my interrogation

over dinner. "Several weeks pay and a glowing recommendation. Always."

"Even for the sous chef who accidentally gave everyone food poisoning?" I pressed.

"Oui. Even for him."

It sounded like Montrose had been treated more kindly than he had any reason to hope to be. Would he still be angry enough to kill someone? He certainly had motive in Baldwicki's case...

"Maman," Nadine said quietly. "What about the woman who wrote that awful review? Didn't Papa end up ruining her? Finding out she wasn't a food expert at all?"

Antoinette waved a hand as if to dismiss this line of thought.

"She pretended to be a food critic?" Diantha asked, and I was glad she'd pressed the topic since I felt I'd probably worn out my good will with the questions I'd already asked.

Nadine nodded. "Evidently. And she wrote a terrible review of Papa's new restaurant right after it opened. It made him so mad, he hired someone to dig into her background, it turned out everything on her resume was either a huge stretch of the truth or a straight-out lie."

"Wow," Diantha said, her eyes huge. "So she had to take the review back?"

Antoinette chuckled then, catching all our attention.

"You cannot take something back once it has been printed."

"So what did he do?" Diantha asked.

"He found other ways to secure her apology," Antoinette said.

"Antoinette," I said softly, wishing there was some easier way to ask what I needed to know. "Do you think she could have done this? To put an end to the... apology giving?"

My friend bowed her head and took a deep breath, which sounded rough, as if she was holding back a tidal wave of emotion. When she raised her eyes to us again, she looked around the table with tears standing in them.

"I told him it was time to end it," she said softly. "That we didn't even need the money. Not really."

Amal and Diantha exchanged a look, and Nadine was staring at her mother.

"What are you talking about? Were..." she seemed to gather herself then. "Were you and Papa blackmailing her?"

Antoinette didn't respond, but dropped her eyes to her plate.

"You have to tell the police," Nadine said.

"It is a motive," I agreed.

"We'll tell them tomorrow," Nadine said, looking around the stunned table. "I'll see to it."

We were all quiet then, the mood at the table having

shifted slightly with too much talk of murder and blackmail to make chicken pie taste quite as good as it had at first.

"I am tired," Antoinette said, rising. "Thank you for everything. I am sorry to bring this trouble to you." She met my eyes then. "But I am grateful for a trusted new friend."

Nadine rose as well, thanked us, and then went with her mother out to the inn, and presumably up to the Atticus Suite for the night.

"Wow," Diantha said.

"Wow is right," Amal agreed. "Should you call the detective?"

I thought about that. It was after eight in the evening, and I'd already woken him twice this weekend. I didn't imagine he was in bed just yet, but I did suspect he might be enjoying a few last moments of weekend leisure, and I didn't want to interrupt again. "I'll speak to him tomorrow," I told them, a little giddy tumble in my stomach as I thought of his low voice in my ear when I did.

Ridiculous.

We cleaned up, said goodnight to Amal, and settled in for the night.

Monday morning after I'd cleaned up the lobby and wished Diantha a good day at school, I was just about to settle onto the couch and dial Owen when my phone lit up with an incoming call. Owen.

"Good morning," I said, answering.

"Morning, Dahlia," he said, sounding a little breathless. "You have a good weekend?"

I thought about that. In the past, my weekends had been silent affairs, full of baking and crochet, walks with Taco and preparations for the week ahead. This one had been very different from that—part of it was being an innkeeper, but a lot of it was thanks to the people who now populated my days and nights.

"I did," I said honestly. "Thank you."

"Well, listen," Owen said. "I know you're probably pretty busy over there with the inn and everything, but I wondered if you wouldn't mind playing detective a bit more today. Baldwicki's lawyer is coming in at eleven and I think I've got Montrose coming with him."

"Oh, yes, I can do that."

"Great," Owen said.

"I was just about to call you actually."

"You were?" Owen's voice lifted hopefully.

"I spoke with Antoinette about the food critic."

"And?"

I looked around the lobby, not wanting my friend to

hear me speaking about her. "I'll fill you in when I see you. Should I come by the station?"

"Yep. How's 10:30? That'll give us a bit of time before they arrive."

"I'll see you then," I said.

"Thanks, Dahlia."

I put down my phone and looked over at where Taco lay, tipped over on one side with his legs out in four straight lines in front of him. He raised his big head to look at me, as if he could sense my eyes on him.

When I said nothing, he let out a soft groan and dropped his head back to the floor.

Amal arrived and assured me she had no need of me until check-in later in the afternoon, so I wandered the apartment a bit, looking for something to do. The sweater I was making for Albert was nearly finished, so I sat down and focused on that for an hour until it was time to head over to the station. I'd just tied off the final stitch when the alarm I'd set chimed.

"Taco," I said to the big brown lump who had followed me into the apartment and then resumed his previous nap at my feet. "Time to go."

Suddenly wide awake, Taco jumped to his feet and began shifting his weight from side to side in excitement.

Chapter Seventeen

The police station was a small building set up a row of wide steps on the east side of the street at the top of the gentle slope where Saltcliff on the Sea was situated. Inside, a lengthy desk stood in front of a single police officer who tilted his head curiously as Taco and I entered.

"Hello," I said.

"Hi there. How can I help you?" The man's red mustache moved when he spoke, and I tried not to stare at it. Facial hair had always been a topic of some interest to me. What led one man to trim it one way and another to do something different? I knew there were cultural roots at play in some of the traditions, but modern facial hair seemed arbitrary to me. It was, I supposed, a bit like women painting their fingernails or swapping out lipstick colors.

"Ma'am?" The man prompted.

I'd gotten distracted with my thoughts about his mustache.

"Oh, yes. Sorry. I have an appointment with Owen."

At the lowering of his furry brows, I corrected myself. "Ah, Detective Sanderson."

The man's blue eyes shifted to Taco and then back to me, and then he picked up a phone behind the desk and said, "Detective, there's someone here for you. And a dog."

He returned his attention to me again, and then pointed to a row of chairs against the wall by the front door. "You're welcome to wait there."

"Thank you," I said, but before I could turn to head toward the chairs, Owen appeared from a door to one side of the desk.

"Dahlia. Thanks for coming in."

"Of course," I said. Owen wore his usual uniform of dark jeans and a button-down shirt with the sleeves rolled up. This one was a shade of green that I noticed made his matching eyes spark in a surprising way.

Owen led me through the door and down a hallway to his office, which had a long window along one wall and held a desk and two chairs facing it.

"Can I get you anything? Coffee?"

I shook my head. "No thank you."

He waved me into a seat, and then sat behind his desk. "So," he said. "The food critic?"

I nodded. "They were blackmailing her."

Owen's brows lifted.

"She lied about most of the credentials on her resume. The chef hired a detective after her pan of his restaurant, and threatened to expose her, I guess. Antoinette admitted it."

Owen nodded. "I'll need her to tell me the same thing," he said. "Good work, Dahlia. You're a natural at this." He smiled broadly at me, and my heart gave a very distracting flutter inside my chest.

"So that's a real motive," I said, wanting to put together all the loose ends we'd collected so far.

Owen's lips pressed together in a straight line. "It is. The question then becomes one of opportunity. And given the weapon of choice, I'm inclined to believe these two deaths are connected, so another question is whether she had a similar motive for Mr. Baldwicki. And did she have the opportunity required for either man?"

"Are you going to bring her in?"

He nodded. "I'll get McKenzie working on it." Owen picked up the desk phone and punched a button and then asked someone to see if they could track down Sally Trenton, the food critic and have her come in today.

"How is Antoinette doing?" Owen asked.

"She's pretty upset," I told her. "Which I guess is what you'd expect."

Owen frowned and dropped his eyes.

"I don't think she did it," I said, the words ejecting themselves before I'd even planned to say them.

The green eyes found mine again, and Owen tilted his head, smiling. "No?"

"They were so in love," I said, surprised at the passion in my tone. I cleared my throat, dropped his gaze. "I mean, that's what everyone said."

"Could be," Owen said. "But being in love doesn't change the fact that she had opportunity and motive with Baldwicki, and certainly had opportunity with her husband. Not so sure about motive there. You overheard that conversation in the bathroom where Mr. Baldwicki said he'd been at the chef's house, right?"

I nodded. I hadn't thought of that. It did give Antoinette an opportunity to doctor a drink or food, I supposed. And she'd had the castor bean plant.

My stomach turned. Suddenly, things looked rather dark for my friend.

"But Montrose isn't out of the woods," Owen went on. "And that's why we need to get some more information from him today."

I nodded. "He had access to the chef," I said, thinking through the things Owen had enumerated when talking about Antoinette. "So that's opportunity. And he and Mr. Baldwicki were old friends, so it's possible they'd seen each other recently."

"Baldwicki ate at the restaurant almost every day," Owen told me.

That was new. "So that's opportunity."

He nodded.

"And as for motive..."

"The chef fired him. And for Baldwicki, it will depend on whether there were hard feelings between them. It sounds like Baldwicki tried to make up for things by giving him gifts here and there."

"Would that be enough to make up for missing out on the only business opportunity to actually pay off after years of effort?" I wondered.

"And did Montrose have access to ricin?"

"It seems like it's available on the internet if you know what you're looking for," I reminded him.

Owen nodded, his face grim.

The phone buzzed then, and a voice let Owen know that Montrose had arrived with Baldwicki's lawyer, who he had evidently retained himself when he realized he might be a person of interest.

"See them to the interrogation room, please," Owen said.

It struck me then how kind a man the detective was. I had never heard a word from him that wasn't polite and gentle—whether he spoke to me, to my dog, to his colleagues, or to a suspect. It was admirable, I thought.

"Shall we?" Owen rose and pulled his office door open, waving toward it as Taco and I rose.

We stepped into the hallway again and Owen led me toward another door on the opposite side of the building. Inside this one was a very small room with a glass window and a desk in front of it. A door stood to one side of the window, and through the glass I could see two men sitting at a table, waiting.

"They can't see or hear us in here," Owen told me.

"It really is like on TV," I noted.

He grinned. "It is."

"Shall I stay out here?"

He nodded. "Focus on Montrose, okay? Watch his expressions and listen carefully to what he says. You may pick up something I don't. Everything will be recorded, too."

"Okay." I pulled out a chair and sat down as Owen stepped through the other door. Taco sat at my side, glancing between me and the window before us as if he wasn't quite sure what we were up to.

"It's okay," I told him, giving his ears a quick rub. "We're just helping."

Taco didn't lie down. He seemed as intrigued by our new role as investigative helpers as I was.

Owen began by greeting the men, and the one I didn't recognize introduced himself as Joseph Hammermill, Baldwicki's lawyer.

The first few questions Owen asked were general, about where Adam had worked and what he'd been up to since leaving the Cliffside.

"I'm taking some time off," Adam responded. "To figure out what I want to do."

Owen nodded, wrote something down. "Does that make it tough to pay rent, though? You live in the townhouses over in Daring Cove, don't you? Rent's pretty spicy over there, I understand."

"This is California. Rent is spicy everywhere," Adam replied.

Owen nodded, then fixed him with a look. "I'm asking what you're doing for money if you're not working."

Adam glanced at the lawyer, who nodded.

"I recently came into some funds," Adam said. "My friend John left money to me in his will."

"John Baldwicki?" Owen asked.

Adam nodded.

"Why would he do that?" Owen tilted his head and fixed Adam with a stare as the other man shifted his weight.

"I don't know, I guess... I guess he felt bad."

"About?"

The lawyer leaned forward slightly and then began speaking. "My client made a very successful business deal on the heels of several failed ventures, of which Mr. Montrose had been a part. Mr. Montrose had lost a fair amount of money in efforts to help my client find economic success."

"So he left him everything because he felt guilty?" Owen asked.

Adam squirmed, but the lawyer remained still. "Correct."

"John Baldwicki had no family at all?"

"A sister," the lawyer said. "But they were not close."

"What a lonely life," Owen said, almost to himself. Neither man responded.

"Tell me a bit about some of these previous businesses," Owen suggested to Adam.

What followed was a long accounting of multiple failed business ventures in everything from day trading to selling kitchen gear.

"The smoothie thing was total luck," Adam finished. "And by then, I guess I'd just lost faith. And a lot of money. I told John I was gonna get a real job. But by then I'd spent all my time trying one thing after another, and didn't have much experience at anything but failing. So fast food was the best option."

"How'd you end up at the Cliffside?" Owen asked.

Adam lifted a shoulder. "John. He was part owner."

Owen nodded. "And did Chef Teratine know you had no kitchen experience beyond fast food?"

Adam shook his head. "John didn't give him much choice about things. He was majority owner."

"Right," Owen said, scrolling through something on his phone that I assumed must be his notes. "And what was that arrangement?" He directed this question to the lawyer.

"What do you mean exactly?"

"How was the ownership of the Cliffside structured?"

"My client had a fifty-two percent share."

"And," Owen went on. "In the event of his death?"

"That share was to be made available for purchase, with the first option of acquisition going to the minority owner."

"Chef Teratine," Owen said.

"Yes," the lawyer agreed.

"Had the chef made any moves to buy that share? After Baldwicki's untimely death?"

The lawyer nodded. "He'd begun the process, yes."

"Acting pretty expediently," Owen said. "Had he ever tried to buy Baldwicki's share before that?"

The lawyer nodded. "Several times, but my client had no interest. In fact, he planned to buy out the chef."

Neither man said anything else. Owen suggested to the lawyer that he didn't need anything further from him, and walked him to the door. The lawyer bustled through the little room where I sat, seeming not to even notice me on his way back out to the hallway.

"Hey, Adam," Owen said, pulling up something on his

phone and then setting it before the other man. "Can you identify this plant?"

Adam sagged. "This again? I made a mistake, man."

"Just have a look, please."

He peered at the phone.

"No idea," Adam said.

Owen picked up the phone, holding it for a moment at an angle so I could see the castor bean plant clearly on his screen. "Ever hear of ricin?" he asked then.

"Sure," Adam said. "Poison."

Owen nodded.

"Have you been in contact with any ricin in the last few weeks, Adam?"

Adam sighed and shook his head. "I didn't poison anyone on purpose." He sounded so utterly miserable, I was inclined to believe him, but I knew that wasn't exactly the way detective work was done. "And it wasn't ricin. It was some kind of weed. Camas something."

"So," Owen said, leaning back in his chair. "How often did you and John Baldwicki see one another after your last failed venture?"

"Now and then," Adam said, lifting a shoulder. "We were friends."

"From high school, right?"

Adam nodded.

"Can you tell me about that friendship?"

The sous chef sighed and looked down for a moment.

"We were kids when we met, you know? And I wasn't exactly the homecoming king, if you know what I mean. But John and me... we were alike in some ways. And we got along well. He kept me out of trouble, too—my brother, you know... he ended up in jail. And I would have too, but John was always coming up with new ideas. Things that were going to make us rich."

Owen nodded.

"He was good with people, you know?" Adam said, hitting his rhythm with the story now. "He could talk to them, making them see things his way. He was a salesman. And I didn't have anyone else. He was my friend, but he was also kind of my family."

To my surprise, the man choked up then, and a sob escaped him.

"Dammit," Adam said, wiping at his face. "I'm gonna miss him."

Owen sat quietly while Adam sniffed and wiped at his face.

"Did you know he intended to leave everything to you?" Owen asked then.

Adam's gaze jerked up. "No! I swear, I had no idea." After a moment he added, "But it's like I said—we were practically family. He didn't have anyone else either."

"You had no idea," Owen repeated.

Adam shook his head. "None."

"Okay," Owen said, standing. "Anything else you want

to tell me? Anyone you can think of who might have had something against your friend John?"

"Only the chef," Adam said. "He hated him."

Owen sat back down. "Yeah?"

"He grumbled about him all the time in the kitchen, called him names and things. He couldn't stand that John came in to eat almost every day and called the Cliffside 'his restaurant.'"

"Why did Teratine go into business with a man he hated?"

"I don't think he had a lot of choice. John saw that place go up for sale and was going to buy the whole building and then lease it out, but the chef showed up at the same time. John said the chef couldn't put together enough money to make a higher bid, so John struck a deal with him, giving him the option to buy the bigger share eventually."

Owen nodded.

"Did John say anything else about the chef? Or vice versa?"

"Not really," Adam said. "John was loud and obnoxious sometimes. He was proud of what he'd built. I couldn't blame him... but the chef always thought he was showing off, and that he just came into the Cliffside to rub his nose in it. I honestly didn't have a lot of time to pay attention to it all. I was trying to keep my job."

"But it was tough with no experience?"

"Really tough. Especially that stupid forage-to-table thing. The chef would send me to his house to pick herbs, and I had no idea what I was looking for. The internet was the only thing that saved me until that stupid onion issue."

Owen nodded sympathetically.

"I didn't like chopping and cooking anyway," Adam confessed. "And now, I guess I don't have to do it."

"Right."

The room was silent a long moment, and just as I thought Owen was going to wrap things up, Adam added one more thing. "You'll catch the guy, right? John wasn't everyone's favorite, but he didn't deserve to die."

"We'll do our best," Owen promised. "I'll walk you out." The two men rose, and walked through the door opposite to the little room where I sat, and I waited in the darkened room, wondering if I was supposed to get up and step out, or if Owen would return. I was just about to leave, when the door opened again and Owen leaned in.

"Hey," he said. "Sally Trenton's here. Got time for one more?"

These interviews had proceeded much more quickly than I'd anticipated, and I still had hours before I needed to be back at the inn. "Sure."

I sat back down as Owen disappeared through the door again, and I waited until he appeared again in the interrogation room, a dark-haired woman at his side. He ushered her to the table, where she sat. She wore bright blue plastic framed glasses and a rather shapeless beige cardigan sweater, which she kept tugging around herself.

"Sally," Owen said, his genuine smile appearing then and visibly relaxing the woman. "Thanks a lot for stopping in. I just had a few questions for you today about your relationship to the Cliffside restaurant and the chef there, Emile Teratine."

The woman's face puckered, as if she had tasted something sour. "I see."

"Are you aware that Chef Teratine is dead?"

"I'd heard a rumor. Small town, you know."

"So you live here in Saltcliff?"

She shook her head. "Salinas. But word travels."

"Was it a relief to you, to hear about that news?"

Sally frowned. "Why would someone's death be a relief?"

Owen leaned back in his chair. "Well, I'd expect that with the chef gone, you might be able to save a bit of money now. With the blackmail coming to an end and all?"

It was the most direct I'd heard Owen be in an interrogation, and I found myself leaning forward, nearly pressing my nose to the glass in anticipation of the food critic's response.

She sighed. "I didn't do it," she whispered, her spine sagging as she stared down at the table. "I might have thought about it over this past year, but I didn't kill anyone." Her chin came back up. "Plus, I'd probably have to take them both out to make it stop."

"Who is 'them both'?" Owen asked, his head tilting.

"Emile and his wife. They were a team, you know. She was more antagonizing than he ever was, coming to my house, pointing her long fingernails into my face and threatening me."

"I think we can assume that's over now," Owen assured her. "I'll see to it if she has any other ideas."

Sally nodded.

"Can you tell me what started the whole thing?"

"The chef was not a fan of my review of his restaurant."

"And he was able to blackmail you because—"

The woman twisted her neck from side to side as if relieving some stiffness. "There were a few inconsistencies he uncovered on my resume."

"Such as?"

"Just small little stretches of the truth. Everyone does it. I needed to look accomplished to get the job at the paper."

"But if they were just little stretches, then why would you be bothered at having them revealed? Surely it wasn't worth paying the Teratines to keep hidden?"

She didn't respond.

"How much did you pay them over the course of this arrangement?"

"Thousands," she said bitterly.

"Must have been something you really didn't want to come out, huh?" Owen was asking the question again, but it he seemed so sympathetic, like he was on her side. I wondered if they trained detectives to do that at detective school.

"I'd never work as a food critic again," she said. "And it's my calling. I'm good at it."

Owen pulled out the resume we'd found in Chef Teratine's office. "So... Culinary Institute of America... is it typical for food critics to go to culinary school? I looked up the standard qualifications for your job, and that wasn't mentioned at all. In fact, the only requirement seemed to be the ability to write expressively about food, and maybe a bachelor's degree in journalism or English."

Sally sighed. "It's not a requirement. But the position with the Central Coast paper was super competitive."

"So you made your credentials a bit more impressive and hoped they wouldn't check."

"They didn't. He did."

"Because you gave him a bad review."

She lifted her chin. "The steak was tough and the swordfish was raw. The food was awful."

Owen nodded. "Made you pretty mad, I bet. Being called out like that when you knew you were right."

She stiffened. "I didn't kill him."

"I didn't even say it was murder, Miss Trenton."

"But it was, right?"

"Had you seen the chef recently? In the past week?"

She shook her head. "I dropped the money at the restaurant when I knew he wouldn't be there. That's what we'd arranged."

"Cash, I'm assuming."

"No trail," she agreed.

"When's the last time you were face to face with Chef Teratine?"

"The day he and his wife came to my house to threaten me. About a year ago."

Owen was quiet a long moment, typing a note into his phone. "And were you acquainted with John Baldwicki? The majority owner of the restaurant?"

Sally tilted her head. "No."

I sagged. If she didn't even know Baldwicki, she most likely didn't kill him. Of course, it was possible these two deaths weren't as tied together as we were assuming.

"Okey dokey," Owen said, rising. "Well, I'd suggest a quick edit of your resume so this doesn't happen again."

"You're not going to out me?" Sally stood, wringing her hands.

"I don't have any reason to. Lying might be unethical, but it isn't exactly illegal."

She visibly relaxed. "Thank you."

"I'll let you know if we have any more questions for you," Owen said, walking her out.

I waited, and a moment later he opened up the door once more, waving an arm for Taco and I to step out. We walked together to the front of the station, and he held the door open for me. "I'll be right back McKenzie."

"Gotcha," the mustached man replied.

"I'll walk you back to the inn and you can tell me what you think," Owen said.

We strolled slowly down the shaded sidewalks of Saltcliff, the sea breeze filtering through the trees. Taco stopped now and then to sniff something along the flowered fence lines, and Owen and I talked.

"I don't really know what I was looking for," I told him. "But I was left with the impression that neither of them really did anything wrong."

"Lucky break for Montrose," Owen said.

"Yeah, that's true. But I really don't think he knew about it. And he just didn't seem like the kind of guy who'd kill his only friend for money."

"I tend to agree with you, and without any hard evidence... we're a bit stuck."

"Antoinette's in trouble, isn't she?"

Owen didn't answer right away, but then he stretched his arms up over his head and yawned. "Man, I don't know. If it were just Baldwicki, I might be tempted to believe she'd had a hand in it. That she and Emile were working together. But with Emile gone too, it just doesn't make any sense. Every account

I can get my hands on agrees that they were totally devoted to one another. Even Sally's story backs that fact up."

"It does," I agreed, relieved that we weren't headed to the inn so Owen could arrest my friend.

We strolled in comfortable silence the rest of the way back to the inn, each of us lost in our thoughts. When we stopped in front of the little garden gate, Owen turned to me.

"Thanks for all your help."

"I'm not sure I've been any help at all," I laughed, feeling the blush beginning to creep up my chest at his sharp gaze. Nerves bubbled inside me and I had the urge to run. Or vomit.

Why was I like this?

Taco pressed himself to my thigh.

"When this is all over," Owen said, pushing his aviator shades up so I could see his eyes. It seemed like he might say something else, but before he could, I heard myself begin speaking.

"Yes, that will be good. When it's over. A relief for everyone." My mouth had opened and words kept rushing out, as if I was doing my best to keep Owen from saying whatever he might be about to say. My hands fumbled with the latch the gate, and as soon as it opened, I practically ran away from him up the path to the inn. "See you later then, okay, bye!"

I pressed through the front door and closed it behind me, out of breath and shaky.

"What in the world?" Amal asked from the desk, her eyes wide as she looked between Taco and me. "Was something chasing you?"

What the heck had I done that for? I didn't have a single good reason in my head, and now that there was a solid wooden door between us, I wished I'd given Owen a chance to finish whatever he had been about to say.

"Not exactly," I told Amal.

She laughed and shook her head, then looked out the window behind the desk. "Owen looks confused," she said, looking back at me.

"I'm sure he is," I told her.

I missed my sister more than ever in that moment. She had known how to handle people. Men. She was good with them. She would never have bolted because she thought someone might be about to ask her out.

But that had always been the difference between Daisy and me. Sometimes I thought it would have made more sense if we were one complete human being instead of two inadequate halves.

Chapter Eighteen

Monday evening, I wove in all the loose ends from the sweater I'd made for Albert the Greyhound and walked it over to Tessa's house.

Loud music emanated from within, and when Tessa came to answer my knock, she was holding a deck of cards and her neck was draped in scarves and crystals.

"Oh!" she said, as if seeing Taco and me on the doorstep was a great surprise. But then she said, "the fates alerted me to your presence."

Odd.

"Um. Okay. Also, maybe the knock on the door?"

She shook her head. "The music is far too loud to hear a knock."

Just then a short man with round glasses stomped out of the cottage next door. "Tessa, goll-darnit! Could you turn the ruckus down already?"

Tessa rolled her eyes and waved me inside behind her as she moved to a black box on a shelf and turned a knob, bringing the decibel level down significantly. "No appreciation for classic rock, that man," she huffed, setting the deck of cards on a card table that stood in front of an armchair.

"Rolling Stones?" I guessed. I wasn't great with identifying music, but I knew I'd heard that band before.

"You got it," Tessa shot me a smile. "I'm getting us a drink," she said, and headed into the kitchen. Albert, who had been curled onto a dog bed near her chair, stood and followed her into the little kitchen at the back of the cottage.

"That's all right, Tessa, I..." But my hostess was already shoving a glass full of ice and something brown into my hand.

"My own recipe. A little southern moonshine and some tropical fruit juice. It'll knock you on your caboose!" She cackled, and I considered this new side of Tessa. She still wore the flowing garments, but inside her own home, she seemed much more relaxed and friendly than she had the few times I'd met her before.

"Take a load off," she said, pointing to the other arm chair. "I'll read for you."

Read for me? No one had offered to read to me since I was small. I wondered if this was some bit of social protocol I'd missed entirely.

But if I expected her to pick up a book, I was disappointed. Instead, she picked the cards up once again after taking a long swig of her drink. "I'm gonna ask you to shuffle these," she said, holding the deck out to me. "Infuse them with your essence."

"I... what?"

"Just shuffle, Doll."

"Okay." I set my drink down and shuffled the cards as Taco wandered over to say hello to Albert. As I moved the cards between my hands, I told Tessa, "I really just stopped by to drop off Albert's sweater. I finished it."

"Oh, that's so nice," she said, laughing. "You hear that, buddy?"

Albert turned his head to look at us, but then went back to sniffing around his bed with Taco.

"Thank you for that. We'll have a look in just a moment here. Now just lay those cards down and cut the deck while you ponder."

"What should I ponder?" I asked.

"Life. The universe. Who's dropping bodies all over town. That sort of thing."

"Tessa," I asked, realizing the cards were quite ornate on the backs. "Are you going to tell the future?"

"Well I didn't light all these candles for my health," she laughed.

There were a lot of candles burning around the front room of the cottage.

"Do the candles help?" I asked. I did not believe in future telling, but the idea was still interesting.

"They put me in the mood," she said. "Now concentrate."

I wasn't sure what I was meant to concentrate on, but Tessa was bowing her head over the deck and resting her hands in the air just above it, so my mind wandered a bit. To very bright green eyes, to a genuine smile, to broad shoulders...

"Okay, let's do this." Tessa spread the cards, laying a few out into a cross, and then she began to flip them over, muttering to herself and occasionally crying out, "yep!"

"So here," she said, pointing to one card. "This is the question."

The question appeared to be some wombats holding up a big cup. "Are those wombats?" I asked her.

"Not the point, Doll."

Was that a familiar nickname or did she call everyone Doll, I wondered. It wasn't my favorite, but Tessa's current attitude did not encourage question asking.

"So you've got the four of cups. And that's what you're thinking about."

"Wombats?"

She looked up at me and squinted. "Daisy always said you were the smart one."

Oh.

I decided silence might be the best way to accept the fortune Tessa seemed determined to offer me.

"You're stuck. Thinking about things. Not sure if you want to take what's being offered to you."

"Oh. Well—"

"You can talk when I'm done," Tessa snapped.

The next card she flipped was meant to represent the past, followed by the present and the future. She ran through them so quickly I wasn't quite sure what I was meant to know from these, but I did notice that wombats were a running theme.

As Tessa flipped the remaining cards, which she'd arranged in the shape of a cross, I looked around the small but cozy space. There were several quilts laid across a lumpy couch that faced a television set. Next to that was a plant stand with a small bookcase beneath it. I didn't recognize any of the titles of the well-worn novels that occupied it.

"Focus," Tessa snapped, noticing my eyes wandering.

"Oh, sorry."

"Okay, look," she said finally, her finger dropping onto a card that showed several small critters (wombats, assumedly) raising their chubby arms up to a bigger wombat who seemed to be rising into the sky. "Judgment."

"Oh, yes," I said, hoping my vocal encouragement would stave off any further reprimands.

"Struggle. Decision. Choices."

Well, that pretty much summed up just about everyone's life, didn't it? And yet, there was something within me that wanted to believe Tessa Damlin could tell me something I needed to know. Some crucial thing that would give me a shortcut to understanding the unexpected turns my own life had taken recently.

"Right," I said, encouraging her.

"This card, and these around it, mean you're working toward something. And you'll have to choose how you do that. You can work with others—accepting help and support where it's offered. Or you can toil alone."

I nodded. Toiling alone sounded lonely. And all too familiar.

"But you will need to make a choice. Soon." Tessa pointed to a darker card, where a wombat appeared to have been flung from a lighthouse. I suppressed a shudder.

"Oh," I said. "Okay."

"Yes okay," she agreed. When her eyes remained on me, I got the sense we were finished. I squirmed a bit and finally opened my mouth.

"Well, okay. Thanks. For. Um... for that."

She scooped up the cards and stacked them together again. "Albert, let's see this sweater!" As she called his name, both she and Albert rose. I pulled the sweater from the bag I'd tucked under my chair.

The sweater was made to look like a letterman's jacket, a pattern I'd found a while ago and modified. The sleeves were deep royal blue, and the collar had a blue stripe, while the main part of the jacket was a cream color. The name "Albert" was written in script across the back.

Tessa stared at it, and then at me, her mouth open slightly.

"You made this." It was not a question, so I waited. "You did not make this."

"Yes, I did."

"You made this."

"Yes," I said.

"Well, Doll, you could sell these for tons of money over at the Mutt Modiste!"

"The Mutt Modiste?"

Tessa nodded, examining the sweater more closely before looking back up at me. "You'd be shocked what people will pay for ridiculous things for their dogs. This is the town for it, though!" She hugged the sweater to her. "I love it. Thank you. Albert loves it."

"Thank you," I said. "For being so welcoming."

Tessa looked up at me, and to my shock, there were tears standing in her almost-gray eyes. "You and you sister... you're good people," she said.

"Thanks."

"Come over soon and I'll take you to the modiste. We can show them Albert's sweater—maybe he'll even model it. I'm sure they'll want to carry these!"

I wasn't sure how much I wanted to make sweaters for

a living, but I usually had a project of some kind going, so I figured it was worth a chat. "Okay, thanks," I said.

Taco and I headed back to the inn slightly dazed—possibly from the moonshine cocktail, but more likely from the strange fortune-telling and the clear, unfettered friendliness Tessa had displayed.

I stepped through the door of the inn, feeling a bit fuzzy all over, to find Antoinette and Nadine reading on the couch, Diantha curled into a chair, and the Levins playing Scrabble at the side table. The Levins were a tiny elderly couple from New York. When they had arrived, they'd specifically asked for the "haunted room" and informed me they were on their fortieth honeymoon. I wondered how the ghost upstairs figured into their romantic plans, but the realized I probably didn't want to know.

"Amal went home," Diantha said, looking up from her phone as I walked in. "She said to tell you good night."

"Thanks," I said, walking to the desk and making sure there was nothing needing my attention. I felt, in some ways, like a real innkeeper now. I knew what kinds of thing we did most days and could probably keep the place running, even without Amal. Which, I thought, gave her a chance to take a vacation or some time away if she wanted. I enjoyed her company, and had no plans to send her packing. But something about the woman seemed...sad.

"Dahlia, would you like to sit for tea?" Antoinette called from the side table where she was pouring a cup for herself. "It has been lonely, being cut from my usual life. And without Emile." A big sniff followed this statement, making it impossible to refuse.

"Of course," I said, moving close to select a mandarin ginger for myself.

We sat as Taco nosed at Diantha for any potential crumbs—he seemed to have discovered that she was a bit less careful than I tended to be with dropped items from the dinner table.

"What have you been up to?" Nadine asked as I stirred my tea.

I was still feeling a little fuzzy from the strange experience at Tessa's. "I think I just had my fortune told," I said.

"Did you?" Antoinette's eyes rounded. "And what have you learned?"

"Do you believe in that sort of thing?" I asked, laughing lightly.

Antoinette looked affronted, jerking back slightly. "I do not question messages from beyond. There is much about this world that we cannot understand, Dahlia."

I nodded, not wanting to dive into my need for logic

and evidence in all things. "Right. Well, Tessa next door did a card reading for me and gave me a drink, and I guess I'm still a little confused," I said.

"What did she predict, Aunt Dolly?" Diantha peered over the top of her phone.

"I'm not even sure," I admitted.

"Many times, the spirits offer only guidance in enigmatic forms," Antoinette said, nodding sagely.

"Right. Well." I sipped my tea. "How was your day?" I asked Antoinette and her daughter.

Antoinette sniffed and shook her head.

"Maman is sad," Nadine said simply.

"Of course," I said.

"To think," Antoinette said, leaning in. "I made him breakfast just a few days ago. Mixed his pills into the oatmeal and sent him off, just like any other day. And now..." she stifled a dramatic sob. "He's gone."

"You mixed his pills into his oatmeal every day?" I remembered being told that the chef couldn't swallow a pill—one of those odd little facts that sticks in one's head, I supposed.

Antoinette nodded.

"She'd been grinding up his heart meds and keeping them in a powder jar since I was a child," Nadine supplied.

"It was easier," Antoinette said. "He would forget if I didn't do it. Or he would mix in too much, or..." She dropped her head and took a deep breath.

"I'm so sorry," I said, uncertain what else to say.

We drank our tea in silence after that, and I sensed that my presence was as comforting as any words I might use to fill the silence. And I'd learned from experience that the words I said weren't always taken the way I meant them. Silence, in this case, was good.

Eventually, we said goodnight and I headed inside with Diantha and Taco for bed.

"Did Albert like his sweater?" Diantha asked before heading into the bathroom.

"I think so. Tessa suggested I show them to the Mutt Modiste and sell them."

Diantha's face broke into a grin. "That's a great idea!"

"I just don't know if I want to have to make so many. It's been a fun pastime, not a job."

The smile faded only slightly as my niece's eyes narrowed a bit and her head tilted to one side. "What if you taught me how to make them?" she asked. "And maybe I could sell them?"

It wasn't a bad idea. "You'd like to learn to crochet?"

She nodded enthusiastically.

"Then yes, of course I'll teach you."

My niece bounced a bit as she disappeared through the door to the bathroom, and I exchanged a look with my dog. His expression told me he was skeptical of my teaching skills, but I thought it was worth a try.

"Dahlia!" Owen said with a smile as he bounded up the steps in front of the station.

The morning had dawned gray and cold, and Taco and I had taken a long walk through town, pausing at the Mutt Modiste to see what kinds of things they had on display in the windows. Considering the fact that dogs did not strictly need to wear clothing, I thought it a bit odd that they shop sold pajamas and formal attire for all sizes of dogs, but it did seem that canines received rather special treatment here in Saltcliff. They had their own spa, after all!

"Good morning," I said, blushing already, though Owen had only said hello so far. "I hope you don't mind me stopping by."

"Never," Owen said. "Want to come in? Is this official detective business or a social call?"

"Er... official," I said, suddenly feeling it might have been the wrong answer, based on the way we'd left things.

"Then let's go in and get some coffee," he said, leading the way.

We followed him, greeting Officer McKenzie and his mustache again as we headed into Owen's office.

Owen fixed himself a cup of coffee and offered one to me, which I waved away.

"Okay, then," he said, sitting. "What's up?"

"Did your men take any samples from the Teratines' kitchen?" I asked.

"Samples?"

"Items for testing? That kind of thing?"

"Let's see," Owen said, turning a monitor to face him more fully and tapping a few keys. "Yep. They did. A mortar and pestle, a jar of powder labeled "heart," two knives, and a cutting board—all things that were on the counter at the scene. They're in processing at the lab."

"Is there any way to hurry that up?" I asked.

Owen raised an eyebrow. "What's going on?"

"I have a theory," I said.

"Let's hear it."

"Well, last night Antoinette reminded me that Emile Teratine couldn't swallow a pill."

Owen nodded.

"And she liked to take care of him, to dote on him. So she ground up his heart medication and kept it in that jar—the powder your team took, probably. And then she put the right dose in his oatmeal each morning."

Owen chuckled. "You know, when you say 'for better or for worse,' you really don't think about all the possibilities, do you?"

"I don't... I mean..."

"So, you think she added some ricin to his oatmeal?" Owen asked.

I shook my head, but then stopped, realizing that was exactly what I thought. "Yes, but not on purpose."

"You think she accidentally poisoned him?"

"Maybe?"

Owen leaned back in his chair. "Walk me through the logic."

"She talked about how the chef never cleaned up after himself, remember. So what if the day he had Baldwicki over, he did poison him? What if he ground up castor beans in his own kitchen?"

"With the mortar and pestle his wife used for his medication?"

I nodded.

"Not super smart, but…"

"Well, if he was the kind of guy who'd fastidiously wash it out afterwards, maybe it wouldn't have mattered."

"But he wasn't."

"Not according to his wife and daughter. Or the state of his office." My mind ran through the possibilities.

"So maybe he also wasn't the kind of guy who thought about that sort of thing…"

"Right. So what if he did that and left it, and maybe there was some left over? And Antoinette might have thought it was his medication?"

"So she put it into the jar where they kept that."

"And then stirred it innocently into his oatmeal the next morning?" I suggested.

Owen was quiet a moment, and then he picked up the phone on his desk. "Hi. Yeah, can we get a rush on that mortar and pestle you've got, and the jar of powder?"

"You think I might be right?"

"It's the best guess we've got right now," Owen said. "And we've got the source of the ricin already at the Teratines' house—or Taco does, at least..." he trailed off, clearly thinking. "But we still don't have a way to prove the chef did it in the fist place."

"I've never been in a close relationship," I said, thinking. The words were out before I realized how ambiguous and ripe for misunderstanding they were.

"Okay," Owen said gently.

"Like the Teratines seemed to have, I mean." My face was on fire. "The love. I mean. The...they were close, right?"

"By all accounts, yes. And I will admit, I'd seen them out here and there, and there wasn't a time I didn't see them holding hands, whispering to one another."

"What I'm trying to say is, do you think he would have done it without telling her?"

Owen stared at me. Then he smiled and his mouth opened. "I bet you're right."

"So if there's ricin in that jar and on the mortar and pestle..."

"And if Antoinette is willing to expose her husband..."

I shook my head. "She won't. She loved him. She wouldn't want his memory to be tainted by something like murder."

"Of course, if it means she won't go to prison for the crime, she might..."

"But Owen," I said, my brain spinning. "Wouldn't she maybe be more willing to say he did it then? Just to keep herself out of jail?"

He blew out a long breath. "You're right." He crossed his arms, bringing on long finger up to tap his chin. "We need to get her talking, without fear of any consequence. We need her to tell us what really went on before Baldwicki died."

An idea took shape in my mind then... a thought about how I might inspire Antoinette to share what she knew about her husband's involvement in Baldwicki's death without thought of consequences.

"Owen," I said, rising. "I have to go. Will you call me about the lab results?"

He nodded. "I'll let you know." As he walked me out, he asked, "Dahlia, what are you planning?"

"I'll call you in a bit," I promised. "I might need help."

Chapter Twenty

Tessa Damlin seemed surprised to see me on her doorstep again so soon, but when I shared a cup of coffee and my request with her, her surprise turned to glee.

"I can do that," she assured me. "I'll enjoy it. Though it might ruin my reputation as a reliable psychic." She frowned at this.

"Do you have a reputation as a reliable psychic?" If she did, I didn't know about it.

"No, not that I'm aware of."

"Then no harm done," I suggested.

She lifted a shoulder. "I suppose not." Tessa walked me to the door. "See you at seven tonight."

I headed back to the inn, working through ways I might convince Antoinette to join in the plan.

It turned out to be simpler than I'd imagined. Diantha

was off to school and Taco and I were in the lobby, cleaning up from breakfast when Antoinette and Nadine appeared. Antoinette all but threw herself down on the sofa, one arm over her eyes as if in a swoon.

"Antoinette, are you all right?"

"Mais, non," she wailed.

I knew she was grieving, and I was certainly sympathetic. But we had such different ways of processing our sorrow and grief, I wasn't quite sure how to react.

Nadine looked as if she'd been crying too, and my heart squeezed in sympathy for both women.

"Can I get you something?" I asked gently.

Antoinette sat up and wiped at her face. "Mornings and late nights are the hardest," she said sadly. "I think of all the times Emile and I were together, the way he cared for me, let me care for him. I just do not see how I will go on, never speaking to my love again..."

"Maman," Nadine said softly, taking her mother's hand.

"I'm so sorry," Amal said, moving to join Antoinette on the couch.

"You said you believed in the messages from beyond that Tessa offered me yesterday, right?" I asked.

Antoinette turned her head to frown at me. "Oui. I do not question things bigger than all of us."

"Do you think maybe Tessa could help you speak to

Emile? Get closure?" It felt slightly wrong to use Antoinette's grief to manipulate her over to Tessa's, but then again, maybe it would actually bring her some peace.

Antoinette seemed to think about this, tilting her head to the side.

"Maman, you should," Nadine said, still gripping her mother's hand. "Maybe Papa can tell us who did this."

"Or at least give you a chance to say goodbye," Amal said, nodding encouragingly.

"Do you think she would be willing to try?" Antoinette asked. "Tessa is... not always agreeable."

"I'll ask her," I offered. "Should we say this evening? Maybe around seven?"

Antoinette nodded miserably, and Nadine rose, giving me a grateful smile as she went to make a cup of coffee for her mother.

"I have an errand to run," I told everyone. "I'll stop by Tessa's on my way and see if that works for her."

"Merci," Antoinette said softly.

Taco and I headed outside and went straight to the police station, where I told Owen about the plan.

"A seance?" he said, shaking his head. "You really think she'll buy it?"

I lifted a shoulder, unwilling to tell him that even I thought there might be things we couldn't quite explain about life beyond this one. "She's given every indication that she does believe in things like psychics and ghosts, yes."

Owen smiled at me and then shook his head softly. "You're really something, Dahlia."

"I am?" I stiffened.

"It's clever," he said, explaining. "Good thinking."

I relaxed under his praise. "Thanks." Then I considered. "So if she says something incriminating because the spirits prompt her to tell the truth, do I need to record it or something?"

Owen shook his head. "In California, you have to be pretty careful. You can't record someone without their consent."

"I suppose she would find that odd, wouldn't she?"

Owen lifted a shoulder. "If the medium tells her she will record the session for her as part of the service, odds are good she'll consent."

"Oh, that's true."

"And if she consents, then anything recorded will be admissible as evidence."

"What if she doesn't?" I asked. Taco looked up sharply at my tone, as if even he was concerned about this possibility.

Owen tapped his chin, and then smiled. "It's not illegal for a policeman to record someone without their knowledge if it is done in pursuit of a solution for a crime."

I shook my head. "I'm not a policeman."

Owen laughed and his green eyes twinkled as he sat across his desk from me. "No, but I am, Dahlia."

"You want to come? Won't Antoinette find that odd?"

"I could be in a back room."

I thought about that. Tessa's place was small, but there must've been a bedroom I hadn't seen. "Would you be able to record from that far away?"

"We can place a bug before she arrives, and if she doesn't consent to recording, I'll activate the recorder. If she does, we won't need it."

I nodded. "Okay. That makes sense. Should we go explain the plan to Tessa?"

Owen rose. "Let's go."

That evening at six-thirty, loud music started up over at Tessa's cottage. I could hear it from the front garden where Taco was having his evening stroll among the flowers. I did not plan to take him with me next door, since Tessa's place was so small and we already had quite a crew attending. Diantha and Amal had asked Antoinette if they might come too, and she'd agreed.

That meant Taco would be staying home on his own, so he got a little extra time out with just me before the big activities of the evening began. It was better this way. If I stayed inside, I was almost sure my awkward inability to behave normally would reveal my plotting.

Good thing I wasn't a murderer. I'd never be able to keep it a secret.

I had just walked Taco back into the apartment and come back out the door when Antoinette and Nadine came down the stairs. Diantha, who had been waiting eagerly on the couch, popped up. "Ready?"

Antoinette nodded, looking a bit uncertain. "I hope Emile will feel me trying to reach him," she said.

"I hope so too," Amal told her.

Together, we all headed next door. As we moved up the front walk toward Tessa's little cottage, the door swung in and Tessa appeared, draped in a flowing floral housedress, her head wrapped in a scarlet scarf and her neck draped with crystals.

Oh. Well. She was definitely taking her role seriously.

"I've made my mystical punch," she informed us, waving us all inside the small space, where we crowded against one another.

Tessa's table was where it had been the night before, but now there were several more chairs arranged around it, and a crystal ball set in the center, which I thought was perhaps a bit too much. She had already turned down the classic rock a bit, and I wondered if that had been Owen's suggestion. I knew he was here, quietly hiding somewhere in the back room. I pictured him sitting on the edge of Tessa's bed, waiting with headphones and some kind of recorder.

"Please, sit," Tessa said, waving us all into seats around the table as she deposited tall glasses of the same moonshine concoction she'd given me in front of each of us.

Diantha picked hers up and sniffed it, raising an eyebrow and considering the glass like she might be about to drink, but handed it to me without question when I stretched a hand across the table.

Tessa moved around the room, lowering the music further and dimming the lights, lighting several more candles.

"I feel the spirits with us already," she said dramatically, and I worried she might be hamming it up just a bit too much until Antoinette let out a little stifled sob.

"Emile," she said softly, and Amal dropped a comforting hand to her shoulder.

Finally, Tessa sat down and laid both her hands flat on the table top. She looked at each of us for a long moment, not saying anything. The delay sent my stomach flipping in all directions, fear and nerves combining as I pondered all the ways this might go wrong.

"Antoinette," she said after a moment. "Do you submit to a reading?"

"Oui," said my friend sadly.

"I will record the reading for posterity," Tessa said, setting a recorder at her side.

Antoinette said nothing, and I worried that we needed explicit consent, so I said, "Oh yes. Recording is just fine with me. A good idea. Is it fine with everyone else?"

Around the table, everyone said yes, and Tessa turned on the recorder.

I imagined Owen relaxing in the other room, though hoped he was still listening. I was certain he was.

"Very well." Tessa handed Antoinette the cards, only after moving the crystal ball to the floor where Albert sniffed it curiously before curling into a pile next to it. She gave Antoinette the same instructions about infusing the cards with her essence and focusing on her question, though Antoinette seemed to be taking the whole scenario much more seriously than I had.

Finally, Tessa had laid out the same formation of cards, and began flipping over those in the straight line. The first card she turned was "the lovers," and Antoinette stifled a sob.

"Ah yes," Tessa said, less dramatic now that she was back in a familiar role, I suspected. "We consider the lovers. Relationships present, past, future—intimacy and secrets shared."

She moved to the next card, hovering her hand over it a beat longer than I would have expected. I glanced up to her face, and felt a little surge of worry when her eyes flew open wide and she cocked her head.

"What?"

"What?" Nadine asked, leaning in.

"But he... " Tessa looked around at all of us, then cocked her head again. "Oh yes, he is here."

"Who?" Antoinette sat up straighter. "My love? Is it Emile?"

"Shhh," Tessa said sharply, waving her hands at us all. "He is whispering. It's very hard to figure out what he's saying."

She shook her head lightly and closed her eyes, bowing her head forward. "No. No, he's gone."

Another sob escaped Antoinette and her hands went to her mouth as her shoulders shook.

Amal shot me a look over her hunched form, as if to ask if this might be a bit cruel. I was feeling the same way.

"Maybe just go through the rest of the cards?" I suggested to Tessa, but she gave me a wide-eyed look, and if I hadn't known how this was all supposed to go, I would have thought she was actually frightened.

She cleared her throat and went back to the reading. "Yes," she agreed, her voice steady again. "Let's.

Tessa went through several other cards, discussing how Antoinette's deep relationship with Emile had colored every aspect of her life, and illustrating with her wombat cards how the woman would have many choices to make going forward. Just as she was about to explain the card at the center of the cross, she stiffened again.

"He's back," she hissed to us all.

Diantha's hand found mine under the table, and my heart squeezed as I wrapped my fingers around hers. "It's okay," I whispered.

It was a bit disconcerting, the show Tessa was managing to put on. It was as if someone really was speaking to her, and she looked every bit as terrified as I would be if a voice came from nowhere suddenly.

She was shaking her head now, and looking at Antoinette. "I don't... I don't understand," she said.

"Understand what?" Antoinette asked in a whisper.

"He says... he says not to hide anything now. He says not to protect him."

"Oh Emile!" Antoinette was openly crying now, tears dragging dark makeup down her cheeks.

Tessa was an excellent actress.

"He is saying he loves you, that you must go on." Tessa paused. "I don't understand this part. It is French, I guess."

"What?" Antoinette sounded nearly desperate, and even Nadine, who had remained stoic most of the time I'd known her, was crying softly.

"He says, '*Entre deux cœurs qui s'aiment, nul besoin de paroles.*'" Tessa's eyes opened wide and she whispered, "I don't even speak French!"

Antoinette let out another wretched sob. "Emile," she moaned.

"What does it mean?" Diantha whispered to me.

Amal leaned over and translated, impressing me as Antoinette continued crying softly. "Between two hearts in love, no words are needed. I've heard it before. A famous quote," she said.

"It is Marceline Desbordes-Valmore," said Nadine. "She was a poet. My parents used to tell each other this constantly."

Well. That was something. Tessa had certainly done her research.

Tessa was sitting stock still, and I was beginning to worry that this act was taking a toll on her as her skin was pale and a visible sweat had broken out on her forehead. She leaned toward Antoinette now and whispered, "*La verite, mon coeur.*"

The lights in the room actually flickered then, and an eerie silence settled. The music, I realized, had stopped. Diantha and I exchanged a look and she squeezed my hand tighter.

"Maman?" Nadine asked, her own expression worried and tense. "What does he mean?"

Antoinette sat up and shook her head lightly. "He wants me to tell the truth. Only, I fear to taint his memory. My sweet Emile."

"What truth, Maman?"

Antoinette drew in a deep breath and then looked at her daughter. "Your papa needed his restaurant. It was the very air that he breathed."

Nadine nodded and I braced myself. This was it. The truth.

"But that man would not release his shares, even when we offered more than the value. Even when I offered… more."

"Maman!" Nadine looked shocked and I wondered if Antoinette really had offered to sleep with Baldwicki.

"I did not have to," Antoinette said quickly. "And I was glad, but I would have. For your papa."

"Ew," Nadine and Diantha both said at once.

"He was not a pleasant man," Antoinette went on. "All those green drinks. They made his breath stink of rotting eggs and kale."

I felt my nose wrinkle in response to the thought of it.

"After asking him many times to be reasonable, Emile was forced to take unreasonable measures. He did not tell me until days later what he had done—he didn't want to involve me."

"What?" Nadine said, her voice shaky now. "What did he do?"

Antoinette's posture stiffened further and she lifted her chin. "He killed him. That is all."

"That is all?" Nadine shrieked. "What? How? How could he do that? Maman, that's murder!"

Antoinette shook her head. "He had little choice, and I do not know exactly how. I only know that he did. He put something in his drink when he came to the house. And then a few days later, we learned that the shares would be released, and we could buy them. But now..." Antoinette's voice trailed off. "Now he is gone." She sniffled, and then bent over her arms again, crying once more.

Nadine appeared to be in shock, tears running freely down her face as she stared straight ahead.

I exchanged a look with Amal, who rose to her feet. "Antoinette, Nadine? Why don't I walk you back to the inn? This has been... this has been a lot. Thank you, Tessa."

Tessa nodded, still looking a bit surprised at the turn of events herself.

"Why don't you go with them," I suggested to Diantha. I could see she was about to protest, but I added, "please give Taco a treat and put him to bed? I'll check in with you when I get back in just a moment."

She sighed and rose to follow Amal and the ladies to the front door.

When they were gone, Tessa stared across the table at me.

"The coast is clear," I said loudly.

Owen appeared from the back room and moved to the table, where he sat at my side.

"That was quite a performance," he told Tessa.

"But that's just it," she said. "It wasn't."

"I mean... it worked," I pointed out.

"But you don't understand," Tessa said, her voice nearly a wail. "I don't speak French. And I don't channel dead people. But that guy—Emile—he was right here, clear as a bell, whispering in my ear." She picked up her moonshine and downed it in one long gulp.

Chapter Twenty-One

It took a long time for Diantha to settle after the odd turn of events and Antoinette's confession of what Emile had done. I didn't calm down right away, either. Because regardless of what the chef had done to Baldwicki, it still didn't explain how Emile Teratine had ended up suffering the same fate. Unless my hunch was right.

When the phone rang on my bedside table before seven, I knew in my gut that it would be Owen.

I sat up, confirming my hunch, and answered.

"Good morning," I said, wishing my voice didn't sound quite so creaky and rough.

"Rise and shine," Owen said. "We've got the info back from the lab. The guys worked late last night."

"I feel like we all worked late last night. That was so strange," I said, but then my mind urged me to get the information Owen was surely calling to share. "So? What do they say?"

Owen sighed. "The powder in the jar of heart medication was tainted with ricin. And the mortar and pestle too. I think your suspicions are correct."

"Oh no," I said, thinking of Antoinette. "Owen, how will she handle this news? She's already in pieces."

"The news that she accidentally killed the man she loved so completely? Can't imagine she'll take it well."

I thought about that, wishing I could think of some way to help Antoinette with this. But of course I couldn't. "No," I said. "She won't."

"Dahlia," Owen said, and I could hear a thought forming by the way he drew out my name. "You don't think there's any chance this wasn't an accident, do you?"

The question surprised me, and I felt my brows lower as I considered it. "No," I said quickly. "Do you?"

"Not really. Just wanted to consider the possibility. I don't see any motive."

"I don't think she had one. I think Antoinette's life is diminished with Emile's death, not made better."

"Her name isn't even on the restaurant," Owen said. "I looked into it this morning. And from what my guys dug up, there was no life insurance on the chef."

"Poor Antoinette," I said. "This is so awful."

"On the other hand, we solved a murder," Owen said.

"Is it anti-climactic if you don't have anyone to go arrest?" I asked, leaning back into the headboard.

"No, not really. I never love that part of things. Someone's life is ruined, you know?"

"Well, if they killed someone, that's two lives ruined really."

"So just desserts, maybe?"

I shrugged, even though he couldn't see me. "I guess in order to do something like that, you'd have to believe it was justified, right?"

"I've heard it said that every villain is the hero of his own story."

"Right." The word came out low and drawn out because the whole discussion made me sad. For someone to feel desperate enough to go to the lengths Emile Teratine had... and for his wife to end up paying for it all in ways he could never have imagined.

"Dahlia?" Owen's voice came through the line again, making it clear I'd drifted with my thoughts a bit.

"I'm here."

"Should I come over? To give Antoinette the news?"

I considered. "Is her house still a crime scene?"

"No, I suppose not."

"Better to tell her there, I think. Let her be home, surrounded by her things. And Emile's."

"You're right. That will be better. I'll come by before

noon to take her and Nadine back to their house. And tell them then."

"Okay. I'll see you in a bit."

"Okay." I heard Owen suck in a breath. "And Dahlia? Thanks for everything."

"Thank you," I said.

We hung up and I sat for a long while, letting my eyes catch on the swaying branches of the Eucalyptus tree out the window. I thought about time and morality, what a strange thing this human life really was—how fragile and how precious.

I was about to get up, realizing my dog and niece would both need feeding soon, when there was a tap on the bedroom door.

"Aunt Dolly?"

"Come in," I called.

The door burst open and Taco and Diantha all but tumbled through it, both of them looking like they'd just woken up. Diantha climbed onto the other side of the queen mattress, and after a moment's consideration, I said, "Okay Taco. Come on," and Taco leapt up too.

Diantha got under the covers and Taco nestled between us, and we just lay there together—the three of us—for a long while as the sun colored the sky brighter shades of blue.

This, I thought to myself, was what it was like to have a family.

That morning I made a quick batch of iced orange scones and some cinnamon quick bread before frying up bacon and sausages to take out to the lobby.

Diantha headed out to school—with noticeably less makeup on, I noticed—and I filled Amal in on my early-morning conversation with Owen.

She sighed, shaking her head. "Poor Antoinette," she said. "You never really got to see them together, but they were a wonderful couple."

"It sounds like it."

"It's rare," Amal went on. "To find someone willing to understand all of you—to let you be who you are and love you anyway."

I watched Amal's face shift as she said this. It took on a dreamy, faraway expression before she took a deep breath and shook her head lightly.

"This shirt," she said, taking the flowing hem of the tank top I'd tugged on this morning between her fingers and then letting it drop. "It was one of Daisy's favorites."

A thought was nagging at me—a question I wanted to ask, but just as I considered whether it would be too personal, I heard Nadine and Antoinette coming down the stairs.

Both of the women looked as if they'd been crying, and I could hardly imagine how upsetting the recent events had been for them both.

"Good morning," Amal said, moving to greet them. "Let me get you some coffee and breakfast. Why don't you sit?" She waved them toward the spots they'd often claimed on the couch and went to get their things.

"I have good news," I told them, taking the armchair next to the couch. "Detective Sanderson says you'll be able to return home today. He'll stop by to let you know when it's ready."

Antoinette nodded sadly. "That is good." Her gaze lifted to mine, just as Nadine asked a question.

"When will we learn more about the suspects in Papa's case? The detective must be working on that, surely? If they're done at the house, does that mean they've found something?"

I wanted to wait for Owen to tell them the truth, but it also felt wrong to know the answer and not share it. I grasped for the right words, but wasn't finding anything. I was about to tell them everything when Amal interrupted by setting down two cups of coffee.

"And your food is right here." She returned with two plates, and I managed to rise and move away to help other guests, escaping the conundrum.

Owen arrived not long after the plates had been

cleaned, and my heart tried to climb into my throat again. We had to tell them now...

"Ready?" Owen asked me quietly at the registration desk.

"I'll call them down." The ladies had returned to their suite after breakfast. "You'll tell them?"

"Of course. You've done enough, Dahlia."

I nodded and then called the suite, letting the ladies know Owen was here and they should bring their things down to go home.

Amal had gone to change out a few rooms, and the lobby was empty when the Teratines came down the stairs with their bags.

"'Allo Detective," Antoinette said.

"Hello Antoinette, Nadine."

Antoinette drew herself tall and lifted her chin. "I assume Dahlia has told you what I shared with everyone last night?"

"About Mr. Baldwicki's death, yes," Owen said, his voice kind.

"Well." Antoinette said, clearly expecting something other than Owen's easy acceptance of the truth.

"The lab has all their results, and we're finished processing evidence at your house. May I give you a ride back?" Owen asked. "I brought one of the cruisers."

"Oui," Antoinette said. She turned to me. "Thank you

so much for allowing us to stay here," she said. She pulled me into a hug.

"Of course," I said. "Should I come help get you settled?"

"No, don't be silly. You have had enough of us."

Nadine hugged me too, and I wished I could come up with an excuse to go with them. What would the truth do to my friend?

Owen gave me a grim look as the women wheeled their bags out, and I gave him a smile I hoped was supportive before heading back inside the inn.

That afternoon, Owen came back.

"How was it?" I asked, already knowing it had to be terrible.

He shook his head. "About as expected," he said. "Antoinette blames herself completely. She broke down. I'm glad her daughter is with her."

"I can't even imagine…" A thought occurred to me then —one loose end not tied up with a neat bow. "But Owen…"

"Oh no. What?" He grinned at me.

"If she didn't know about the ricin, why was she removing the castor bean plant?"

Owen's smile faded only slightly. "I asked the same question. Great minds," he said.

"And?"

"She told me that the chef often planted things for the restaurant, and that he was supposed to put them strictly in the side bed, but that he was lazy about it. She said it was the one thing they fought about—his messing up her perfect garden."

"So she found the plant and just dug it up and tossed it?"

"Right," Owen confirmed. "But I think it's pretty clear why the chef didn't put it in with all the herbs he used at the restaurant."

Of course. "You're right."

There was a moment of silence between us, and my mind went back over all the strange happenings here, landing on Antoinette's unfortunate mistake. "What will she do now?" I asked.

"I don't think she intends to stay here in Saltcliff," he went on, moving to pour himself a cup of coffee. "It sounded like it would be too much—to see his things and the restaurant. She wasn't widely accepted here either, so I'm not sure how supportive people might be."

"Where will she go?" I asked.

"Her daughter suggested they get a cottage in Daring Cove or maybe farther inland, but Antoinette was considering returning home to France, I think.

I sighed. The whole thing made me so sad. "I'm so sorry for her."

Owen nodded.

"Was it awful for you? Having to tell her?"

"Comes with the job, I guess," he said. "Though I'm glad to have this case at its end. Now I can get back to the usual variety of Saltcliff police business."

"What does that entail?" I asked.

"Cats in trees, neighbors arguing about whose tree is dropping fruit into whose yard, that sort of thing."

"Sounds good," I told him.

"And now you can get back to the business of innkeeping, I guess," Owen said. "I'll miss working with you, though. Your mind is very impressive, Dahlia."

"Thanks," I said, feeling the heat in my cheeks already. I'd miss having an excuse to see him regularly too. Maybe I could get a cat and send it up a tree, just so I'd have an excuse to call him.

"Maybe we could go to lunch one day," he suggested. "We would have to find something besides murder to discuss, though."

The blush burned hotter, but I tried to swallow down the nerves flying around inside me. "I'd like that," I told him.

"Me too," he said.

Taco pressed up against my leg as I sat next to Owen. I

could never have predicted how my move to California would turn out, but so far... life in Saltcliff agreed with me.

I couldn't wait to see what happened next.

Thanks for reading the first Saltcliff mystery!

Want to see what Dahlia, Danny, and Taco are up to next? Don't miss Bumped Off at the Bake Sale, the next Saltcliff Mystery! Get it here! And keep reading for recipes straight from the Saltcliff Inn!

Chocolate Chip Oatmeal Icebox Cookies

This icebox cookie recipe has a story. (Really, doesn't every recipe have a story??)

This is the first thing Dahlia bakes in her new home in the Saltcliff Inn, an action she undertakes to comfort her niece, Danny, who she has no idea how to handle (yet).

I chose this recipe to offer comfort and love to Danny because it represents those things to me. It's also ridiculously simple.

This is one of the only recipes I'll share that is actually a family recipe of mine. (That's because my family just doesn't have a lot of 'family recipes' - my mom really didn't cook, and neither did hers, so whatever traditions we might have had were forsaken in my grandmother's pursuit of her work — she was President of the National Education Association at one point — and my mother's general lack of interest.)

This cookie recipe is my great-grandmother's, as far as I know. She had a cabin in Kings Canyon-Sequoia National Park in California, where my mother was raised in the summers, and where my family spent our summers too. My great-grandmother taught Mom to make these cookies, and I had the chance to make them with her several times too (my family enjoys longevity!)

My mom sent these to us when we went away to college, and I've always made them for my kids, and I know my brother makes them too. So now, Dahlia shares that comfort with Danny, and I'm sharing it with you!

CHOCOLATE CHIP OATMEAL ICEBOX COOKIES

Ingredients:

- 1 cup shortening (Crisco)
- 1 cup packed brown sugar
- 1 cup sugar
- 2 eggs
- 1 tsp. vanilla
- 1.5 cups flour
- 1 tsp. salt
- 1 tsp. Baking soda
- 3 cups old fashioned oats
- 1 12 oz. package of semi-sweet chocolate chips

Directions:

- Cream shortening and sugars until smooth and blended; add eggs and vanilla and beat in.
- Stir together flour, salt & soda; add to creamed mix.
- Stir in oatmeal, one cup at a time.
- Add chocolate chips and stir in.
- Batter will be very stiff.
- Roll into three logs, wrap each in waxed paper and chill.

Bake:

- Heat the oven to 350 degrees.
- Slice chilled dough into 1/4" rounds and place on ungreased cookie sheet.
- Bake 8-10 minutes

* If freezing, wrap logs in foil in addition to the wax paper. Can be baked from frozen - no need to defrost.

* I learned this recipe at the cabin, which is at about 6000 ft. No need to modify for high altitude, but if you don't like how the cookies flatten out, try one (or all) of the following:

- Increase the temp to 375

- Decrease the baking soda to 3/4 tsp
- Add a bit more liquid (maybe 1/4 cup milk?)

Rosemary Lemon Tart

Lemon is one of Dahlia's go-to baking flavors. It's bright and refreshing, and with Daisy's garden blooming out in front of the Saltcliff Inn, why wouldn't she toss in just a hint of fresh rosemary? You can make her recipe without the rosemary if you like.

Grab a tart pan (removable bottom types work best!) and get going!

Make the crust first, and then make the filling while the crust bakes.

Crust Ingredients:

- 1 1/2 cups all purpose flour
- 1/4 cup granulated sugar
- 1/2 tsp kosher salt

- 1/8 cup powdered sugar
- 8 tablespoons butter (melted)
- 1 tablespoon water
- 1 tbsp chopped rosemary (optional)

Crust Directions:

- Spray your tart pan with cooking spray and heat the oven to 350 F.
- Whisk all dry ingredients together in a big bowl. Whisk in rosemary, if using.
- Pour the melted butter into the dry ingredients and mix well. Add water as needed to create a dough that looks like big wet crumbles. It will come together, but not into a solid ball.
- Take little bits of the dough and press up the sides and into the bottom edge of your tart pan and then fill in the center with the rest. Press it all into an even layer and then prick with a fork all over the bottom.
- Bake for 10 minutes.
- Press with a measuring cup or glass back into shape gently, pressing the crust against the sides and bottom, then bake again for 5-7 minutes and set aside.

Tart Filling Ingredients:

- 1 1/2 cups granulated sugar
- 1/2 cup all purpose flour
- 2 tbsp cornstarch
- 1/2 tsp kosher salt
- 6 eggs, large
- 6 egg yolks, large
- 1 cup lemon juice, (from 5-6 lemons)
- 1 cup whipping cream (optional)

Tart Filling Directions:

- Preheat the oven to 325 degrees F.
- Whisk the sugar, flour, cornstarch, and salt together in a large bowl.
- Whisk in the eggs and egg yolks.
- Stir in the lemon juice and pour the filling into the crust.
- Bake 30 - 40 minutes or until the edges of the tart are beginning to turn golden. The filling should be slightly wobbly in the center. It won't "look" done, but that's what you want - it'll set up as it cools. If it's overbaked, it'll crack as it cools.
- Top with whipped cream.

Cinnamon Caramel Muffins

Dahlia experiments a lot to create the treats she serves at the Saltcliff Inn. This one started as a plain cinnamon muffin with a streusel topping, but morphed when she thought it needed just a little something extra. She began by unwrapping a caramel square and putting it in the center, but eventually decided it would be easy enough to make her own caramel filling.

The addition of a condensed milk drizzle was Danny's idea, but you'll definitely agree it is exactly what these muffins needed to go from great to spectacular!

Since I live at high altitude, I've also included the modifications I make when I make these at home! (I'm at 6500 ft.)

Before you begin:

Preheat the oven to 350 degrees (375 for high altitude!)

Line a muffin tin with baking cups.

Batter:

- 2 cups all purpose flour
- 2 tsp baking powder (reduce to 1 1/2 for high altitude)
- 1 1/4 tsp ground cinnamon
- 1/2 tsp salt
- 1 tbsp vanilla extract
- 1 cup whole milk (add 1/4 cup greek yogurt for high altitude - nonfat is fine!)
- ⅔ cup light brown sugar firmly packed
- 2 eggs
- 6 tbsp butter (melted)

Filling:

- 4 tbsp butter (melted)
- ½ cup + 2 tbsp light brown sugar firmly packed
- ⅛ tsp salt
- Pinch of cinnamon

Streusel:

- 1/3 cup all purpose flour
- 1/4 cup light brown sugar firmly packed
- 3/4 tsp cinnamon
- 2 tbsp butter (softened)

Optional Drizzle:

⅓ cup condensed milk

Directions:

Batter:

Add all ingredients to a bowl and stir until just combined.

Caramel:

Combine all the filling ingredients.

Put it together!

Add two tablespoons of muffin batter to each muffin tin. Add a heaping teaspoon of filling on top, making sure it doesn't touch the sides. Add additional batter on top until the muffin tins are 2/3 full.

Topping:

Stir the flour, brown sugar, and cinnamon together. Work the butter into the flour mixture with a fork or your fingers until coarse pea sized crumbs form.

Sprinkle a generous amount of the topping on the muffin batter and press lightly to make it stick.

Bake:

Put the muffin tin one one rack and a baking sheet on the rack below it. If the filling bubbles out, it can make quite a mess!

Bake at 350 degrees (or 375 at high altitude) for 17-20 minutes, or until a wood toothpick comes out clean.

Remove from the oven and allow to sit for about 10 minutes and then drizzle with condensed milk.

There'll be more recipes coming your way in Bumped Off at the Bake Sale, Book 2! Get it today!

More Nancy

The Saltcliff Mystery Series:

Book 1: Keeled Over at the Cliffside

What happens when Gilmore Girls meets Murder, She Wrote? You get Dahlia Vale and snarky Diantha along with Taco Dog solving murders in the Saltcliff Mystery series! Follow along as Dahlia builds her community and family, and solves mysteries along the way. You'll love the small town vibe, B&B setting, and romantic sub-plot in this cozy culinary series!

Other Books - Steamy Small Town Romance written as Delancey Stewart

The Wilcox Wombats Series:

Book 1: The Wedding Winger

Ready for some ha ha with your hockey? The Wilcox Wombats bring the camaraderie and sense of found family you're looking for, along with snort-laughs and swoons. The first book features a star winger planning for his future, but caught up in the past. When his high school touch (the smart girl who always thought he was just a dumb jock) moves back next door, he knows he's in trouble. Grab it here!

The Kasper Ridge Series:

Free Prequel: Only a Summer

Book 1: Only a Fling

Read the Kasper Ridge Series to get your fill of small town steam with plenty of humor! Former fighter pilots share deep bonds and plenty of inside jokes. Step into their world as they join together to help renovate the Kasper Ridge Resort, a dilapidated mountain property in Colorado, left as an inheritance to Ghost, one of their own. But the inheritance also comes with a treasure hunt! Each book follows a different couple but each story builds another link in the hunt, so read them in order! Start with Only a Summer, which is free! Then pick up Only a Fling here.

The Singletree Series:

Book 1: Happily Ever His

What happens when the totally normal sister of a movie starlet meets her ultimate movie star crush, only to find out he is dating her famous sister? But it gets a bit more complicated than that.

Tess's sister has brought movie hottie Ryan home for her grandmother's 90th birthday to show the world how quickly she could move on after her very public divorce. The relationship is just for show... but Tess doesn't know that at first. And Gran? Is a video gaming, weed smoking, take-no-prisoners firecracker who tells it like it is. Toss in a lovesick chicken, and you're on your way to understanding what kind of series Singletree promises to be. Plan to laugh. Pick up book 1 here!

The MR. MATCH Series:

Free Prequel: Scoring a Soulmate

Book 1: Scoring the Keeper's Sister

If you enjoy a side of sports with your sexy men, and want both wrapped up in a hilarious package, then you're going to love Mr. Match. Soccer star and genius Max Winchell has discovered the formula for love and built a dating app around it. Though he keeps his identity secret, he convinces all his teammates to try it... and one after another, they fall in love. First up? Fernando "the fire" Fuerte, who shares an enemies-to-lovers romance with PR rep Erica, who happens to be his teammates twin sister. Taboo, forced proximity, and tons of witty banter up the steam in this one! Get it here!

The KINGS GROVE Series:

Book 1: When We Let Go

Coming right up, a bit of Sequoia mountain steam mixed with small town swoon! Head to Kings Grove for quirky side characters, emotional love stories, happy ever afters, and a cast you'll want to make your neighbors. Book 1 features Maddie returning to her childhood home, only to be swept off her feet by a handsome and potentially dangerous stranger. These books are steamy and engaging, with a touch of humor. Read book 1 here!

THE GIRLFRIENDS OF GOTHAM Series:

Book 1: Men and Martinis

Head to to the dot-com heyday of NYC - the late 1990s! Join Natalie Pepper as she makes her way in the big city in this Carrie

Bradshaw meets Bridesmaids coming of age story. Meet the girlfriends here!

The Digital Dating Series (with Marika Ray):

Book 1: Texting with the Enemy

Looking for sweet romance with a romcom kick? That's what you get when Delancey and Marika Ray team up! In this series starter, Elle is texting a guy she isn't sure she likes, but boy does he give good text. The only problem? She's actually texting her boss since "the guy" gave her his buddy's number instead of his own. Now she's falling slowly in love with the perfect guy and can't figure out why he doesn't seem perfect in person... Needless to say, hilarity ensues. Pick it up here!